To Sienna

x

This is Sue Hampton's fourth historical novel, but she also writes fantasy, humour, mystery and contemporary stories and likes to explore the future as well as the past. Sue is looking forward to 2012 London Olympics, which will be rather different from the Ancient Greek Games in this novel and might not be *quite* as exciting!

Keep up with Sue's news on www.suehamptonauthor.co.uk

By the same author

Spirit And Fire (Nightingale Books) 2007
ISBN 9781903491584

Shutdown (Nightingale Books) 2007
ISBN 9781903491591

Voice Of The Aspen (Nightingale Books) 2007
ISBN 9781903491607

Just For One Day (Pegasus) 2008
ISBN 9781903490372

The Lincoln Imp (Pegasus) 2009
ISBN 9781903490389

The Waterhouse Girl (Pegasus) 2009
ISBN 9781903490426

Twinside Out (Pegasus) 2010
ISBN 9781903490457

Traces (Pegasus) 2010
ISBN 9781903490464

Ongalonging and the Snowgran (Pegasus) 2011
ISBN 9781903490471

The Judas Deer (Pegasus) 2011
ISBN 9781903490624

Frank and Zoo and the Wannabe (Pegasus) 2011
ISBN 9781903490648

Hue and Cry (Pegasus) 2011
ISBN. 978 1903490 631

Lap of the Gods

Sue Hampton

Lap of the Gods

Pegasus

This book is dedicated with respect to all the athletes I've cheered.

Chapter One

The slave known as Chorus was strong as a bull, but she had done enough. No man would have travelled further, with greater speed or stealth. Now she could complete her task and forget. The time it took was not for thinking, and Chorus knew better than to wonder what the soothsayer might have said. It made no difference. The baby boy she had wiped clean and wrapped in swaddling bands would not live with his mother, in the house where he had been born a secret. Chorus allowed herself no feelings as she carried the clay pot onto the hillside. Her load was lighter than water or firewood, and once she had abandoned it, there would be no questions.

Still he slept. She placed the pot in the thin shade of an olive tree. Exposed babies lived or died. Whether or not their futures lay in the hands of the gods, Chorus could not say. And never would. Others might laugh at the nickname; Chorus could not share the joke. But she understood very well why she had been chosen to carry the child as many miles as she could walk. It was not only her strength that had marked her out, but her silence. Chorus could neither hear nor speak.

Megacles enjoyed riding, and sometimes it was good to be quiet. The last time he had taken out his favourite horse, he had spent the time listening to his friend Archilochus, who liked to talk. The subject – the wife his friend claimed was mad – had not been to his taste. Athenian men did not, as a rule, talk about their home lives. Megacles would never complain about his own wife, Alcestis, and had no wish to hear his friend rail against the woman she loved best.

"Eurycleia's like a dry twig!" Archilochus had complained. "I don't know whether she'll snap or spark into fire!"

The women were cousins but after Eurycleia had been orphaned as a small child, they had lived as sisters. Their education as girls set them apart from other women. But while Megacles thanked the gods for his wife's cleverness, his friend had a different view.

"A woman's mind is a shallow vessel, with just enough room for domestic concerns – but not for ideas! Eurycleia's been filled to overflowing, like a vat of oil that spills in wind."

Megacles had smiled against his better judgement. His companion liked speeches and at the agora he could always draw a crowd.

"Not that she bothers herself with the practical. She weaves nothing but a world of her own. She's drunk on poetry. And she prays like a priestess."

Megacles had been sympathetic. A mad wife would be a burden, and keep a man from his home. But Megacles loved Alcestis, and had not shared news that would distress her.

Now he rode alone. As he turned homeward, he smiled in anticipation of the welcome she would give him, and pictured the curve of the belly where another child grew. Three had died, but this son was strong, kicked hard, turned and stretched like an athlete in the womb. This one would live.

Perhaps the horse knew before him. Was it the sound, quieter at first than the murmuring of wind in the olive branches? The pot that rested in the shade, half-hidden by a straggle of grass and leaves, was brown as earth.

Dismounting, Megacles looked inside at an infant with eyes closed, reaching a small fist into sunshine. His wife was the thinker. Megacles did not waste time debating the unknowable. Sometimes the simplest of actions was enough. He only unwrapped the swaddling bands to check for missing limbs, for twists or growths. There was no disfigurement. This boy looked strong as well as handsome. The brown eyes could not be finer if Zeus himself had fathered him.

Megacles smiled. They could always use another slave.

There was blood, but Eurycleia closed her eyes on it. What could not be washed clean was burned to black. She did not sleep at first, for the nights were haunted by hungry wolves with tearing jaws. Through her sleep she heard them howling on the hillside but in the mornings they had gone. She turned to her mirror, and prayed to Aphrodite, whose beauty was curved on its handle. While her body healed, she masked the pallor of her face, and wished she remembered how to run.

At the farmhouse Megacles presented the baby like a gift. Alcestis was shocked and upset, then charmed and thankful. She talked, delighting in the child, his eyes, his mouth, his complexion. She smiled, touched carefully, lifted him from the casket and anxiously declared him cold. Holding him close, she wrapped him again in a shawl around the swaddling bands, and then laid him down when his eyes closed for sleep. Megacles looked again at the casket that might have been a coffin. It seemed no more sinister now than the powder pot where his wife kept her cosmetics.

She was looking too, at the word, or beginnings of a word, smeared in dye along the side.

"D... A... M..." read Alcestis, a finger tracing the shapes.

As a shadow fell chill across the room, Megacles felt sudden doubt. Perhaps it was not a name at all, but a curse.

"Damastor," said Alcestis.

The sun returned and shone on her smile. Seeing that it was decided, Megacles did not argue that a name was a luxury a slave did not need – any more than he needed a past.

"Don't get too fond," he said, and as she knelt to stroke the curve of the boy's scalp, he expected no reply.

Chapter Two

Alcestis placed the crown of flowers on her son's head. At three years old, Lysias understood what to do with a yo-yo, a top or a hoop – even if Damastor did all of it faster, with greater ease and control. But these flowers on his head were a puzzle. Unlike his chariot, the wreath could not be pulled along by a string; unlike the ball of tied-up rags, it was not for kicking.

Lysias lifted it from his head and examined it, checking on words to match the colours. Damastor watched. His head was bare, his hair and legs long. He would have liked to hold the flower ring for a dog to jump through. Lysias smelt it, and let loose a sudden laugh. He twitched his nostrils as they filled with scent. Alcestis smoothed his hair and took the wreath.

"It's your crown of flowers," she told him. "It belongs on your head."

A large, flat head it was, and beneath it were large, flat ears that Megacles likened to loaves. Lysias was solid, compact and tough, a small tree trunk of a boy, cut too low to the ground. But it did not give him balance or strength. Damastor was the one who ran, jumped, swung and spun, climbed and rolled. Lysias preferred life slow and upright, yet his days were full of tumbles, scratches and sobs. He submitted to his crown but his eyebrows furrowed.

"I am not a king."

"Indeed you are," Alcestis told him, "King for the day." She saw that he did not believe her and remembered that he preferred truth. "It is to mark the end of your infancy. You are no longer a baby but a boy. And on the second day of the Anthesteria you may join in the festivities, and drink your wine."

Lysias pulled a face. He didn't like the smell of wine.

"Will Damastor drink it too?" he asked, imagining that if there was a race Damastor would beat him to the finish.

"He may, for slaves are permitted," said Alcestis, allowing Damastor one of her smaller smiles before she kissed Lysias on his broad nose.

She led her son by the hand to the dining room. There she looked for Eurycleia, but saw with disappointment and anger that Archilochus had left her at home, like a cloak he did not need. Lysias stared down at the mosaic floor where fish leapt and nymphs carried baskets of olives.

Damastor followed at a distance, and found himself pulled to the side with the other slaves. There were jugs to serve, and wine to mix with water. He saw eyes communicate as slaves' eyes must, without words. He tried to serve Lysias but the jug was snatched away by an adult slave who grumbled that he would be bound spill the wine.

Damastor heard the name of Dionysus, called aloud and echoed in murmurs. Damastor knew Dionysus was a god, and gods were to be praised. But he could see no sculpted figure towering above the guests, dazzling with gold. He could see Lysias puzzling too, his eyes upward to the faces. Damastor knew his friend would rather be outside, digging earth or following butterflies.

The older slaves were swift to serve the crowd. One of them handed Lysias his own little jug, his chous, decorated with fat children playing. Damastor moved to drink from its lip. A silence had settled, so the bugle startled his mouth open. A competition! Damastor understood. He drained his wine, grimaced and wiped his mouth. Then he held up his empty jug. Across the room, in the centre of the celebrations, he saw Lysias burying his head in his mother's skirts.

"Lysias!" cried Damastor. "I win!"

Lysias heard him through all the other voices. The jutting chin softened as he grinned. Damastor would have run to him, but the slave with the fiercest face held him back as he broke away.

"You stay where you are," Theognis muttered, bending down to Damastor, his mouth spraying wine-red spittle on his forehead.

He reached out a hand and cuffed the side of Damastor's head so that his ear began to burn.

"You're a slave. Don't forget it."

Damastor had been struck before. It hurt very little, but sometimes his eyes watered and he had to blink and pull them wide and strong.

Lysias was drinking reluctantly, his father tipping his jug while he struggled towards his mother. His crown of flowers fell to the floor. The cheers, loud and sudden, were not for Lysias but for a guest with flabby arms who had drained his own jug and lifted it high. Stout and ruddy, he called the name of Dionysus, but Damastor could not imagine a man who looked less like a god. His gleaming face might have been oiled after a steam bath. But Damastor respected victory, and joined in the applause. The champion knuckle-dried his dripping chin.

In second place was a man Lysias had seen before and knew to be a friend of his father's. Tall and muscular, he seemed to him more likely than any other guest to be a god in disguise.

"Bad luck, Archilochus!" someone cried. "You're out of practice!"

Megacles slapped the man's back and laughed at something Lysias could not hear. As a fat goose was presented to the winner, Damastor saw that Lysias had wriggled free from his mother. He beckoned.

"Come," mouthed Damastor, smiling, and Lysias grinned.

Needing little encouragement to escape, he began to weave a path between adult legs, but tripped. He knocked the scab from a tender scrape and bit his lip to stop the noise that might disgrace him. He cried, as quietly as he could, while his father led a surge of laughter at his fall.

A puzzled frown was knocked from Damastor's forehead by a heavy hand pushing his chest where the bone felt hard. Damastor was pressed to the wall by bigger, stronger hands that grasped his wrists, while feet kicked his calves and ankles. A knee jabbed him in the stomach. And then Theognis was pulling him up and smoothing him down as if he too had fallen and needed help.

"Can't hold your wine," he muttered, breathing warm and damp in Damastor's ear. "And you with such fast little legs it's a shame to see you lose them."

Meanwhile Lysias butted his head into the folds of his mother's dress. Alcestis coaxed and comforted.

"You're not a baby now, my dear," she added. "Stand tall, shoulders high. No more crying."

Damastor's head and stomach felt full of fire. He stroked his wrists as if to take away the pain. It didn't work, but he'd been hurt enough to know it only took time.

Detached from his hiding place, Lysias scowled at the floor. Megacles turned to his guests, the smile on his public face stranded awkwardly. When he caught sight of Damastor watching intently from a corner, he could not help imagining this other boy in the centre of the room, courting admiration, performing for the crowd and feeding on applause. His father, whoever and wherever he might be, would be proud to stand beside him. And Lysias? With his straw-like hair and spread nose, he might have been a farm boy after an encounter with a bull.

Megacles was worried. In a few months' time the members of his clan would gather from all over Attica to be introduced to his son. Lysias would be registered as a member of the phatria and a citizen of Athens. And whatever Alcestis might say, no one would see the sharpness of his mind.

Megacles emptied his jug and wove his way through his guests, inviting them to talk. He nodded, raised an eyebrow, agreeing and encouraging. But he felt shamed.

Alcestis, meanwhile, had taken their son outside to breathe some cooler air. The wine had made him flushed and nauseous. Glad of the pale, windswept sky and the scents of fruit and earth, Lysias sat on her knee while she stroked his hair. He had not enjoyed the attention any more than Alcestis had enjoyed the company of men.

If this was the world from which wives were excluded, then she was content to live outside it, for she considered it full of fools! The men in her dining room might prize fitness and physique, but it seemed to her that few of them knew how to exercise their minds.

Lysias was pointing, naming, comparing and questioning.

"You will show them," she murmured. "There is more to dignity than muscles. You will outwit them all one day."

October brought the Apatouria. Alcestis was expecting another child, but she could not leave the shopping to her slaves. She took charge in person, rising early to lead them out through the dew to pick the best the market had to offer. It was good to be outdoors, the breeze on her skin, lifting the trails of hair that lay in curls on her shoulder. She felt as if her pulse quickened as she breathed in the air, and listened to the noise as if each sound played a note in a piece of music she had almost forgotten. Though she covered her head in a plain shawl, she felt exposed and rebellious, but curious too.

She would have liked to linger to watch the cobblers, jewellers, furniture makers, the molten bronze cast for a statue and the clay shaped on the potters' wheels. She had heard there were ten tall figures rising above the agora, representing the tribes of Attica, and a water clock that timed the speeches of men. But she could not push Megacles further than his respect could stretch. She did what she had to do, and nothing that she could not justify. She shopped, and bought the best – plenty of it.

The feast was exquisite. Roasted songbirds, tuna, grasshoppers and snails were served along with vegetables, porridge, lentils and olives. There were figs and grapes and honey cakes. The guests were full of praise and Megacles was full of pride. And all in honour of their son, her Lysias, whose right to be a citizen of Athens was to be established and celebrated.

Many of her husband's family had travelled far. Some of them Alcestis had met only at her wedding. Then she was a girl, shy and embarrassed, but with Eurycleia close by to support her. Now she sat between strangers, alone with thoughts she could not voice, receiving their news like a jar presumed to be empty.

Outside, Lysias and Damastor played, their only interest in the horses that had brought guests to the house. Standing on a pile of hay, Damastor helped to feed them while Lysias watched warily from a distance. The animals seemed to him majestic but colossal, their eyes hard to read. But Damastor was unafraid, as if he liked them, and knew that they liked him. When one grey made a disconcerting rumble of a snort, Damastor only patted. Lysias pulled the same face and attempted the same nose-and-throat noise – which ended in a splutter and left him with eyes that watered. Damastor laughed.

"Respect!" he said. "They're bigger than you!"

The horse made another noise from a different place and when Lysias copied that too, Damastor's shoulders shook until the slave groom slapped his face.

It was not until the third day that Lysias was presented. Unhappy that Damastor was not to be there this time, he found himself at the centre of a great deal of attention from which he couldn't hide. Alcestis had warned him to be brave, and when Megacles offered a goat for sacrifice he remembered, and only covered his ears as it bleated under the knife. Blood splashed the mosaic floor. Pressing his lips together with his teeth, Lysias did not cry, although he knew the goat by name and had stroked it only hours before. When the priest was presented with an ear, a side and a thigh, Lysias fixed his gaze above the blood and beyond it, as if his heart was hard. The sacrifice was for him and he must honour it. And when the flesh was cooked and served with cakes and wine, he chewed slowly with his head high as his mother had taught him. His cheeks were clean, his lap free of crumbs and his manners perfect.

"Now, Mother?" he asked Alcestis, when his stomach was full.

But she shook her head and whispered, "Not yet."

Lysias was ready now. The words were threaded in his head and he didn't want to tangle them. When he'd practised, reciting the lines his mother had taught him, he had linked them to Damastor's actions, but now he must manage alone. His father had told him that Damastor would never be a citizen like him.

"Being your companion is one of his duties, that's all, and better for him than scrubbing or emptying buckets. But he is here to do as we tell him."

Now Megacles announced that his Lysias wished to address the phatria. There was a sudden murmur of surprise before the hush. Lysias began his poem. Gods. Ghosts. Animals. Heroes. Hills and rivers. The words were big and heavy, ringing in the silence. He didn't understand them all, but he felt their power. Only once did he pause, the chain broken. His forehead wrinkled. His lips puckered. He felt his audience waiting. But then he called back the picture of Damastor waving from high in a tree. In his head the words he needed waved too, like branches green with leaves. His mother smiled as he delivered them, his confidence surging, to the end of the poem. But his father? Had he pleased him at last?

So young and so eloquent! Such authority! Such a strong, deep voice for one so small! What a feat of memory! How wise he must be to show such understanding! All around Lysias he heard deep voices in praise of him!

Megacles lifted him and held him high, that all could see the child whose voice had commanded them. Lysias reddened in delight at the cheers. Soon Megacles was swearing that he, Lysias was his son, born to him by his noble wife. There were words Lysias did not know and ideas he could not feel. And all of it felt very serious and important and made him serious too.

"Well done, my son."

Lysias felt proud. His father was happy, and one day he would be a true Athenian like him. But before he slept he asked Alcestis about his friend Damastor, who had no father and no mother either.

"Can't he be a citizen one day?"

"No, dear. Damastor is a slave and slaves cannot be citizens."

"Why?" he began, but he knew that was a question he asked too often. "What can slaves be?"

Alcestis had not thought for a long time about the baby in the clay pot who had been replaced by the long-limbed boy. She told herself there were truths that once lost could not be found without digging hard, and that if they were uncovered there might be uprooting, demolishing and rebuilding at a cost no one could guess. He lived and that must be enough.

"Slaves are the property of their master," she told him. "They can be sold, rented or given away."

Lysias was horrified. She saw his alarm, and reassured him.

"Damastor belongs here," she said. "For now."

"Will he be beaten?" asked Lysias, for he had seen slaves flogged. Damastor had seen too. They had averted their eyes and said nothing.

"Slaves may be flogged. It is a punishment."

Alcestis did not mention that the crime might be small. A free man might pay a fine of one drachma for an offence that would earn a slave a lash.

Lysias shut his eyes tight. He did not want to picture his friend bleeding under the whip. But Damastor was so strong! He would fight anyone who tried to beat him!

Alcestis told her son to sleep. She too would hate to see their youngest slave in pain, and thanked Hera that he was a good boy who showed no temper or resentment. Alcestis had argued with Megacles about the ruling that no slave could give evidence in a trial except under torture. It was the way things were, he said, supposing it fit and proper. For Alcestis it was outrageous, brutal and stupid – one of many laws she would unmake, should she be allowed within a mile of the agora.

"You will learn and understand," she told Lysias in a whisper as he closed his eyes, "and then you will look again, and see new truth, and share it."

Lysias was asleep. She slipped away and gave thanks at the altar to Hera for her son, the only one who had lived. And for the first time since Megacles had brought her the baby in the pot, she prayed to the goddess for Damastor. With an offering of fruit, she asked Hera to protect a son who was not hers, but lost to a mother who would have loved him – better than she dared to do.

As winter set in, the house was daubed with pitch. It steamed black as a stallion but to Lysias it smelt worse. Dark and bitter, it filled his mouth. Damastor encouraged him to spit out the taste, but Lysias could not project his spittle so far or so fast. Hesiod, the slave master, gave Damastor a shove, and then a grin, and told him not to teach Lysias manners unworthy of a citizen.

"The pitch is foul," said Lysias, who thought the house began to look as if a three-headed monster might fill it.

"It's supposed to be foul," said Hesiod, allowing himself a smile. "It's to ward off evil spirits."

Lysias thought bad spirits might like bad smells. He was afraid they would gather that night to plague his dreams.

"This is what happened before you were born," Hesiod told him.

"What about me?" asked Damastor.

"Not you," said the slave master, his voice flat now. "You're a slave."

Lysias had been told he would soon have a brother or sister, and didn't mind. But the pitch bothered him. He wanted to make sense of it. And he didn't like the thought of sleeping in a house that pretended to be a cave.

"If evil spirits come, my father will fight them," he said.

"That's as maybe," said Hesiod. "But if I were the master, I wouldn't take any chances. Customs are customs. Best play safe."

The midwife arrived later that day. Alcestis explained to Lysias that he must not be distressed by blood or screams, or by separation, but pray to Hera for a safe birth. He nodded, promised and wondered. Only his mother answered his questions properly, and now he must keep away from her.

He played with Damastor outside, looking back at the pitch-blackened house and afraid to picture the blood that wasn't a sacrifice. He listened for screams, and made ready to cover his ears, but there was no sound louder than the wind.

The next day Damastor tried to stop him brooding by devising a kind of chariot race which involved pulling quails around in carts. But the birds in Lysias's cart were too nervous or too bold to stay on board, while Damastor's passengers cheeped happily as they rode to victory.

The two boys were helping the feathered charioteers from the chariots when Lysias saw his mother's maid hang something outside the house. He thought at first that it might be a lamb's tail, but the wind tugged it into a curling flutter. The boys left the quails to flap and totter to freedom, and ran to find out. Lysias knew it meant something. Sometimes it seemed to him that everything had a meaning, but nothing could be explained, no matter how many times he asked for reasons.

Damastor arrived first. Through the doorway he could see slaves on the move, their paths crossing or dodging in haste. Something was happening. But now that he was beneath the sign he frowned back at Lysias, arms wide, palms upward.

"It's just a strip of cloth!"

Lysias stared at it, yellowy white, torn and plain. He felt a disappointment that was as breathtaking as the run. What could it be? No ribbon for a lady's hair. It was more like a caterpillar ready to crawl away. Was it a bandage? He looked up into the sunlight but he could see no bloodstains. Was his mother safe? He looked for the maid who had hung it there, but she had returned to Alcestis. Damastor asked the few slaves who usually bothered to answer him but this time it seemed they were not telling. It was some time before they overheard that there had been no need for an olive branch because a girl had been born.

"Don't girls matter?" Lysias asked Hesiod.

The slave master seemed amused. He smiled unexpectedly between issuing orders.

"You'll have to work that one out!" he said. "And you won't need your abacus."

"I don't think they do," said Lysias.

He knew that olive branches were for celebrations and victories. Strips of cloth were for cleaning and polishing.

"You could ask your mother," Hesiod told him, and grinned.

When at last he was sent for, he found Alcestis looking flushed and glad to receive him. She reached out to take his hand.

"This is your sister," she said, and a maid brought in something not much bigger than a weasel, wrapped and warm.

Lysias felt a laugh break out, because she was funny and he liked her face, even though her eyes were closed and her skin was wrinkly. She seemed important to him. And perhaps girls mattered in their own way after all, because three days later honey cakes were sacrificed to the gods when his parents named her Corinna.

Chapter Three

Four summers later, Damastor and Lysias were outside the farmhouse. Damastor lowered himself into position, his bare feet tilted up from the dry ground. The goat bleated its objections as Lysias caged it in – with lengths of wood, and a seven-year-old arm that was rather shorter than the planks, and much more bothered by horns.

"Ready?" muttered Damastor, without lifting his head, which faced down to the flat stretch of swept but dusty ground.

"I am!" said a struggling, ducking, swerving Lysias. "I can't speak for the goat."

Damastor smiled, because Lysias could mimic every animal they knew.

"I'm sure you could!" he cried.

Now Damastor must focus again. He tightened, alert and poised, for the race to start. And then, with no word or signal, the goat was free! Lysias was sitting in the dirt, and Damastor must sprint for the bucket at the foot of a plane tree.

"Go!" cried Lysias.

Now that he was seven he laughed at crashes and up-endings more often than he cried. Damastor was running already, unsure whether Lysias was encouraging him or the goat. For the first time he wondered whether the first clue that his shaggy opponent was at his shoulder might be a two-pronged attack of horns in his backside. But the bleating sounded distant. He was ahead, and in the clear! As he kicked the bucket at the finish he threw up his arms, only to find the goat grazing on a stubby sprouting of grass behind the start.

"A real Athenian victory!" cried Lysias, when he'd stopped laughing. "No serious opposition!"

"I wanted a race," objected Damastor. "There's no glory in defeating a goat that doesn't try."

"There's no glory in defeating me either," said Lysias, grinning at the dirt that wouldn't be brushed from his chiton. "You've done it a hundred times. Do you want me to find a pig?"

"Well I'm certainly hungry!"

Lysias laughed. "You're always hungry!"

Damastor liked his food, and his friend made sure he ate better than other slaves, who could only dream of pork. But anyone who exercised as much as Damastor needed to graze regularly, like the goat.

"I'll outrun a horse one day," he boasted.

Lysias laughed picturing it.

"Let's go and see the horses," he said.

When Damastor raced off, he had to chase him. It was Lysias who was meant to be at ease on horseback, but Damastor who could ride with confidence – even though as a slave he only needed to learn the skills of grooming, feeding and clearing the steaming dung.

At the sound of a cry Lysias stopped. It wasn't Corinna, and it wasn't loud, but sharp. Damastor heard in it something he recognised as fear. They looked at each other and hurried towards it. Some way outside the house, where the buckets of urine and faeces were emptied and buried with earth, they saw two slaves arriving. In front was a young female, stumbling as she carried two buckets that stretched her bare arms tight. Behind was the slave they called Theognis, striking and poking her with a long, knotty twig. Lysias and Damastor saw and heard the foul-smelling contents of the buckets swill and spill, and splash her legs and feet along with the hot, dry ground.

Damastor stopped. Theognis wouldn't want to be watched. It wouldn't be the first time he'd been kicked for being there when he shouldn't be. Lysias kept on walking towards them, expecting with every step that Theognis would register him and leave her alone. Instead he grabbed the girl's shoulders.

"Down!" he said, and she set the buckets on the ground. "Kneel!"

He pushed her onto her knees between them. Lysias didn't know what the older slave meant to do next but he knew he must prevent it. Running, he drew close now, but Theognis did not seem to see or hear. Or care.

Lysias stopped right in front of the two slaves but still Theognis did not look up. He pushed the girl's neck forward and jerked it to the side, unbalancing her. She moaned as he pressed her head down against the rim of one bucket. Still she was struggling, her arms wide and helpless at her side, her fingers spread with nothing to hold on to. They heard her retch as she tried to pull away and up to air. But Theognis did not let go of her neck.

"Stop!" called Lysias, standing between the two slaves and the cesspit, the smell still leaking inside him after his mouth shut tight. He thought he might retch too.

Theognis looked up at him, the cruelty slowly emptying from his face. Lysias saw he was thinking. Then he let go of the girl, who whimpered, her shoulders sinking. Lysias pointed to the house and she hurried away, wiping her nose with her fist but ignoring the leg trickled with yellow.

Damastor stepped forward. It was not for him to look at Theognis. Instead he took the wooden handles, and carried the buckets as if they were little jugs full of first wine for infants, until with one movement, he emptied them into the cesspit. Then he carried them towards the house, keeping his eyes ahead. Increasing his stride, he began to catch up with the girl, who ran faster but didn't dare turn round. He would help her wash her tunic if he could.

Theognis stood, legs apart, narrowing his eyes at Lysias. Waiting. Lysias knew it was not his place to give Theognis orders. He also knew that Theognis would not want him to tell Megacles what he'd seen. For a moment the eye contact they held kept both of them still and silent. Then Theognis turned and walked casually away, his swagger reined in as he drew closer to the house.

Lysias wanted to call after him, *Don't do it again!* Or *I'm watching you!* But he was not sure which words he needed and what effect they might have. Biting the inside of his mouth where the right ones should have been ready – to be hurled out like weapons to hit their target – he blew out through his nose and ran to the stables alone. He did not know whether to tell Megacles, or how he would react if he did. More than once he had been cuffed for "insolence" when he disagreed with something his father said. When his mother told him not to mention to Megacles certain things he would not like, they often concerned Damastor. But as a rule his father seemed much too busy to trouble himself with the play of boys.

So it was a surprise for Lysias when Megacles appeared later that day. He and Damastor were running down the hillside, gathering speed as the slope pulled them towards him.

"Father!" cried Lysias, the word breaking into a laugh as he hurtled.

Megacles could not help comparing. Lysias was all angles and jerks and jolts. Damastor was upright, steady, landing on his feet while Lysias stumbled into a roll.

"Lysias," called Megacles.

Lysias pulled himself up from the grass and sheep pellets.

"Father," he said again, more soberly.

"Leave us," Megacles told Damastor, who nodded and broke into a run that gathered speed towards the house.

Megacles dusted his son's clothing to little effect. Lysias smoothed his own hair as best he could.

"Mother?" he cried suddenly, imagining reasons for his father to seek him out. She had borne two dead babies since his sister's arrival and he had seen her sadness.

"Your mother is well," said Megacles, who knew his son was an affectionate boy. No harm in that, but it was time now for less childish concerns. "I have come to tell you that I have been into town today, to talk with the paidotribai."

"A teacher," said Lysias, his tone expressionless. "I am going to school?"

"You are," said his father. "It is time. I have told him that you are already a scholar, and he is looking forward to teaching you."

Lysias thanked him. He did not feel glad to leave behind the hills and animals, or the space to think thoughts of his own. But he enjoyed numbers almost as much as he loved words, and he would like to play the flute or lyre.

The sun was fierce. His father led him to the shade of an olive tree, where they sat silently. Lysias breathed in the air as if he might soon be parted from it. In the distance the brown speck that was Damastor raced away out of sight.

"Will Damastor …?" he began, but his father interrupted.

"You will have a paedogogos, the best of the slaves. He will accompany you to school and bring you safely home again."

"Isn't Damastor the best of the slaves?"

Megacles studied his son as if for the first time. Alcestis had encouraged this. In a slave it would be backchat. In a free man, it would show an independent mind. But a boy should not question his father's decisions.

"He's better than Theognis," added Lysias, wary but determined. "This morning we saw. . ."

"Damastor is too young," interrupted Megacles.

"He is almost as tall as the lamplighter slave," exaggerated Lysias, "who has stubble on his chin. Damastor could wrestle him, and throw him down."

"Damastor has duties here. School is not for him," said Megacles. "And he is not your twin."

Lysias did not mean to laugh but the idea was too funny. One short, one tall. One swift, one lumbering. One lithe, one clumsy. One handsome, and one as rough and bumpy as the earth at their feet. But he was serious again in an instant, his head down.

"Nonetheless," he said, "Damastor is a brother to me."

Irritated, Megacles rose. "Then you have made a mistake," he said, "and you must unlearn it."

His only son had become dependent on a boy with no identity. It was time for Lysias to set Damastor aside, like the top he no longer spun and the two-wheeled cart that had broken long ago. He walked away, leaving Lysias to follow. As Megacles looked down towards the house he remembered the sight of Damastor, tearing away like a stone from a sling. The boy could certainly run.

For Lysias it was the end of his child's curiosity sparking in darkness. Now he found knowledge served up like a feast, and his appetite was enormous. He was quick with numbers and read and wrote well, exercised his memory and enjoyed plucking a tune from the lyre. But he was not the perfect pupil. His dancing was not elegant; he laughed at it before others could, and kept laughing, longer and louder than anyone else. Most of all he disliked boxing, since it involved being struck about the head and chest by hands wrapped in ox hide while trying not to buckle or cry. When it came to fighting he felt like an infant in the dark. He did not need to tell Alcestis. She saw the marks on his face, and soothed them with herbs and water.

"I'm not fast enough," he told her, after another pupil had bruised and torn his cheek. "Damastor would dodge, and catch them off-guard. I just stand with my fists up and hope no one knocks me over."

"Use your strengths," she told him, patting his hips. "Keep yourself firmly rooted. Watch and think and seize your chance. It only takes one powerful blow if it's well timed and well placed."

"I'd rather beat my opponent in other ways," said Lysias, "if I have to have opponents at all."

"So you shall," said Alcestis, patting his hand. "You will debate like a philosopher and no one will defeat you. Wherever you go, admirers will sit at your feet, in awe of your intellect."

Corinna tumbled in, chased by Damastor and laughing wildly. At the sight of her brother's face she opened her mouth in horror and ran to stroke the cheek below the swelling. Her fingers felt to him like the wings of moths, slowing drowsily. He laughed too. Her mother scooped her up onto her lap and addressed her tangled hair, which had trapped twigs and leaves.

"What have you been doing with her, Damastor?" asked Alcestis, who knew Corinna liked his company better than anyone's. "Don't tell me," Alcestis warned him with a smile, "and then I shan't have to ban it."

With dinner guests to provide for, she left the children alone a while, knowing how the two boys liked to swap accounts of their days. As soon as she had gone, Corinna picked a stick from her hair and sat on the beaten earth floor, scraping its smooth surface. Damastor sat beside her, his back straight, his face pulled so serious it made the others laugh loudly. Lysias held up his stylus and wax board, marking out the first letter of his sister's name. Recognising it, she concentrated on its shape as she traced it in the earth with her twig. Damastor copied too, and they named the letter in unison. Lysias recited a passage of Homer that he had memorised that day, pausing between sentences for them to repeat. Corinna's mistakes provoked more laughter from the boys. Far from being offended, she joined in, delighted, and her fists on Damastor's chest were light and playful.

But Lysias stopped, mouth open and head back, at the sound of footsteps he recognised. His wide eyes sent a warning. Damastor threw the twig behind the fire. Picking up the bundled rags that made a ball, he used them to rub away the letters from the floor before throwing it for Corinna to catch. The dust dirtied her dress as she trapped it against her chest. Megacles walked in and found his small daughter playing while his son appeared to be thinking intently, his head tilted upward.

"Looking to Mount Olympus for inspiration?" joked Megacles. "One day you'll get an answer, and I hope it won't be a thunderbolt!"

Damastor was bowing hastily. He slipped away before he could be dismissed. Megacles held out his arms to Corinna.

Her smile was tentative; she hesitated a moment, and he looked hurt that when she did go to him, she didn't run or smile.

"You haven't forgotten me?" he cried, for it had been several days since he had sought her out.

She shook her head. He stroked the swinging hair, pulling a stern face at the leftovers of her outdoor adventures that showered down.

"You're dirtier than a slave from the silver mines!" he cried, pushing her gently away and dusting down her short, play-stained peplos.

Corinna looked at him uncertainly, unable to judge his tone. Was it play or rebuke? She couldn't always be sure. So she was relieved when he asked her to sing, sending for a better player than Lysias to accompany her on the lyre. Soon a musician appeared, one of those hired for the feast, and when the song was finished, he bowed and remarked on the beauty of Corinna's voice.

Megacles nodded. The man would feel obliged to say so, of course. Flattering men like him was as necessary for musicians like this one as keeping his instrument in tune. But he prided himself on his listening ear, and believed he could trust it. For all her dirt and tangles, Corinna could sing like a sea nymph, her voice light enough to dance on water. He felt a father's pride, and kissed her head.

"Bed," he told her.

As he walked away he remembered his philosopher son, and wished him goodnight. After he'd gone, Lysias sighed like a thief who had escaped a flogging.

It was the next morning, as Corinna slept and Lysias dressed for school, that a messenger brought shocking news. Their

38

father's friend Archilochus was dead. Lysias could picture the tall man, the one with broad shoulders and a loud, laugh-with-me voice who had been second in the drinking contest when he was small. He had picked him up once, but then put him down again as if he didn't know what to do with him. Alcestis said Archilochus was married to the woman she loved best, her cousin Eurycleia, who was now a widow.

"What will happen?" asked Lysias, because he guessed that the passing on of an important man would be marked with a ritual, one that would be new and strange.

Alcestis was preoccupied and gave no answer. She felt no sadness. Eurycleia was free of a man who scorned her – and his death would permit her to see her cousin at last.

Chapter Four

The body lay on an elaborate couch, feet towards the door. Lysias remembered his mother's explanation. Bodies were positioned this way so that the spirit could leave – but why would a spirit need a door? Around him mourners gathered to moan quietly at the sight, among them a priest who placed a wreath on the dead man's head.

In her black robes, his mother's skin looked pale, but not as white as the face of the widow. Lysias thought Eurycleia very beautiful, but her eyes were so dark and full they troubled him. He knew he was too old to be frightened of a weeping woman, however wild her wailing, but she made him want to hold his mother's hand and grip it tightly.

There was a boy, perhaps eleven years old, whose skin and neck were swollen and flaky red. He hung back behind the dark-eyed woman, pulling at his dry, raw hands. Lysias guessed the dead Archilochus was his father, and Eurycleia his mother. The boy looked as if everything hurt so much it made him cross as well as sad.

Then, as Lysias stood between his parents, Eurycleia took a knife from a tall slave woman who looked more than strong enough to wield a sword or hurl a spear. Lysias stared as the widow held out the knife like a threat or warning, as if the crowd were an attacking army. Then, drawing it in towards her chest, she ran a forefinger along the edge and licked the blood.

Bright traces beaded her lip. The tall slave with the cropped, man's hair moved as if to wipe the blood away from metal or skin, but Eurycleia's hand warned her to stop. Then she pulled a thickness of her own hair and sliced it away in one stroke, catching a lock with the other hand. Stray curls separated as they fell, to be swept up with a broom by the slave. Eurycleia placed the lock of hair in the still hand of her dead husband.

Megacles whispered to Lysias that his mother must cut her own hair as tribute to the dead. Lysias looked away and wished he had not come. Alcestis touched his shoulder reassuringly before she cut, but what she felt was shock. The silence throbbed into a noise that felt barely human. And Eurycleia seemed so distant and strange, so hard to read, her eyes speaking a language Alcestis did not understand.

Stepping forward to honour the man she hardly knew and liked even less, Alcestis played her part. It was hypocrisy and she hated it, but sometimes it was necessary. She had no wish to be cast out like an evil spirit.

No sooner had she presented the lock of hair than she spun round at a scream behind her. Eurycleia tore at her cheeks with her fingernails, right, then left, clawing through the tenderness of flesh. As her fingers worked, her hair tumbled and swayed with her hips in a kind of dance. Blood trickled from her face down her neck and onto her shoulders; it splashed her chest. A woman standing nearby was sprayed, and received the blood like a gift, smearing it over her own face and beginning to rip at her own skin. In the midst of women wailing and tearing, Alcestis felt trapped. And all the while, flailing closer with each swerve and spin, Eurycleia danced, her hair sweeping the air like wind.

Then she fell, and Alcestis caught her. The body of Archilochus was being lifted into the coffin by brothers and cousins. One of them delivered an oration in praise of the dead man, but it was hard to hear. Eurycleia wept, sinking into Alcestis as the procession began.

Lysias watched the son who followed blankly at the front, and thought how tight and tender his body looked. At his shoulder his mother stumbled, supported by Alcestis. Lysias felt glad of his own soft flesh and his own father, reassuringly solid behind him.

Corinna showed no sign of tiring of the game. Up on Damastor's back, her arms around his neck, she cried, "Faster!" and then, "Faster still!" as he ran with her legs swinging.

Ducking and swerving, he tried to satisfy with thrills as well as speed. She made a light load; it was her bounce that slowed him, and his care. In the absence of the master and mistress, no one had given him permission to carry her, and if he tripped and dropped her, Theognis would kick and slap him harder than ever. Now it would soon be dusk. He must make sure that when the nurse maid looked for her, she was ready to be washed and put to bed.

"I want to be a charioteer," she announced, when he stopped at last with a loud neigh, like a stallion that refused to trot any further.

Damastor laughed. Corinna frowned. He stroked her cheek with a bent forefinger the way she liked. She smiled, but she was not happy with him.

"Come," he said. "Time we were back."

"Why can't I be a charioteer?"

"There are reasons," he said. "Your mother will explain."

She hung back. He waited, but when he walked on she did not move.

"Corinna, please."

"Will you be in trouble?"

He nodded, and she ran, took his hand and hurried towards the house.

"I don't want you to be in trouble," she told him, squeezing his hand.

"I prefer not to be," he said, and held his backside as if it had been beaten – which it had been, by Theognis, no more than a week before. "It hurts."

She looked up at him so sadly that it made him laugh.

"Don't worry about me," he told her. "Soon, no one will beat me again." Without warning he ran like a sprinter at the starting line. "Because no one will catch me!"

Corinna gave chase, squealing.

Night was approaching and the body must be taken out of the city walls to be buried. Slaves held candles along the line of mourners, whose howls reached out into the darkness of the hillside. The wind had a flickering bite as it whipped black wool at bare legs and spread hair around candlelit faces. Lysias felt gripped by silence, as if his mind was numb. Nothing his mother had taught him, nothing he had learned so far in school, had suggested this.

On they walked, the darkness thickening steadily with the miles, the noise lowering only to rise again. For a few moments Lysias could not see his mother, or the widow woman who frightened him. But the head and shoulders of the short-haired slave woman rose above the rest, as if she were a statue in a market place. At last they came to the burial place, not far outside the city walls that loomed like a giant fortress. It was so dark now that nothing had any definition within the blackness, but the air carried its own taste of fruit and ash and oil.

Lysias preferred not to see what was happening. It was enough for him that his father provided a low-voiced account, without the shadows of flame and the blood-scratched faces white in moonlight.

"A fee for the ferryman," said Megacles, as Eurycleia placed a coin in the dead man's mouth, "who will carry him across the river to Hades."

Slaves produced platefuls of food.

"For four days offerings will be left on the tomb," Megacles told Lysias, "and then the dishes will be broken so the ghost cannot come back for more."

Lysias tried to picture Archilochus, between one life and the next, wispy as smoke or thin as a veil of lace. Would he be greyed over bone, and ghoulish? Or would he be unchanged? He imagined the man on the couch slipping out of his skin into a vaporous image of his old self.

Alcestis liked the idea she had seen once in an old tomb, of the soul as a tiny winged figure that became a star, but for her it was simply a fancy. Archilochus might just as well become a sheep, or its droppings. Lysias watched the boy with the fiery face step forward, with the uncle who had given the oration standing behind him.

"Melissus," whispered Megacles. "He has a statue of his father."

The son placed the small carving on the coffin. There was a pause as if he might speak, but he only left offerings around the figure, and slipped back into the crowd. The moaning had grown thin as the smoke from a dying fire. Eurycleia still gripped her cousin's arm, so tightly that Alcestis would have liked to protest. The skin pressed against hers was cold now, her body twitching with shivers.

"Has he really gone?" whispered Eurycleia. "Will he be back to punish me?"

Alcestis guessed he had punished her enough. Not because he was bad, but because he'd had no use for her intelligence, or her love.

"He's gone, sister," she told Eurycleia, "and now we can be together again."

Eurycleia stroked her shoulder and murmured, "That is not to be."

She spoke like an oracle, as if her words carried meanings deeper than anyone but the gods could interpret. Alcestis did not argue. Eurycleia called Melissus. As he returned, his mother kissed the top of his head where there was no redness, no cracks, puffiness or crusts.

"I am punished already," she told Alcestis.

Alcestis shook her head and gave Melissus a smile Lysias knew well.

"Surely you are blessed, sister." She took the boy's hands as she spoke. "Our sons must become friends."

Lysias felt alarmed, then guilty. He would rather play with Damastor, even if he would never be a citizen. It wasn't this boy's fault that his skin burned like hot coals, and Lysias was sorry. But he looked as if he'd had no fun from the day he was born. And in the darkness his eyes glinted, hard as spear heads. Eurycleia pulled her son towards her.

"Poor Alcestis!" she cried, her voice rising above others. "So wise and so clever – and yet you know nothing."

Eurycleia pulled Melissus behind her, and turning away from the procession, began to run. Alcestis watched a moment as the mannish slave followed at her heels. Then she told Lysias to stay with his father, and hurried after them. Widow, son and slave had left the crowd and were heading away from the burial ground, racing with long, swift strides. Only Melissus turned his head as she called. Feebly Alcestis begged them to stop, afraid of the fierce intent that dragged her sister away.

Alcestis heard the water before she saw it: a thin, snaking ribbon threaded with silver. The mourners passed it by, their torches fragmented in its flow. But Eurycleia was running towards it, as if it lured her with its breathy murmur. She shrugged off her black robe and stumbled over stones into the stream, the gleaming white of her skin lost in star-specked black. And there was no splashing, just a surge into bubbles and stillness.

"No!" Alcestis cried out, but her voice fell like a stone.

Her eyes could find no trace of hair or feet, of swollen cloth or air. As girls they had learned philosophy and politics, but had never been taught to swim.

The slave woman brushed past and was in the water before Alcestis had reached the river's edge. Melissus stood impassive, but as Alcestis reached for his hand the fist unclenched to be held. While they watched the slave waded, stooped, thrust out her arms and reached down and around under the dark surface. Soon her chin met dark water as the current tried to push her aside.

"Mother," murmured Melissus.

Chorus dragged her mistress up to the air, hooking her elbows underneath her. Eurycleia's chest lifted and dropped in a rush of water and air. The rest of her clung, thin and draping as cloth. As Chorus stepped out of the river she carried her load ahead of her like an offering to be laid at the feet of the gods.

Alcestis would not forget the faces caught below the moon. Eurycleia, eyes upward to the light, was a girl again, as if lost in daydreams. Crying out without words, the boy tore open like a bud. And the slave called Chorus kept her mouth closed and her eyes ahead.

At the house, Eurycleia slept on the couch where the body had lain. The wailing was muted now; others spoke in sharp whispers as if they shared a scandalous secret. Megacles declared that he must stay to honour his friend, but Lysias could see he was tense with fury, and hear in the words a kind of rebuke. He did not understand. He only knew that he and his mother were going home, but he could see that she did not want to leave. As they rode away, Lysias touched his mother's hand, because under her hood she was crying.

Chapter Five

When Megacles returned home by night almost a week later he clasped his wife's head to his chest. He tried to stroke and soothe but she broke away, her eyes demanding something he could not give.

"Gone? Where could she have gone? Why didn't you go after her?"

Megacles sighed. He had already told her. He told her again. "The brothers and I spent the best part of four days searching for her. She doesn't want to be found."

"You asked at the port? People who saw her wouldn't forget."

"I couldn't rummage around the hold of every ship, Alcestis. You haven't been to Piraeus. You have no—"

"I have no idea. How could I have? And she has no idea either. How will she survive?"

"She isn't alone," he reminded her.

"Melissus is a boy, and sickly too!"

"Not just Melissus," said Megacles, who did not need to be reminded that she had dragged the boy along, separating him from everything that was his birthright. "She took that slave they call Chorus."

It was a comfort of sorts. Alcestis remembered the strong arms that lifted Eurycleia from the river. But it was not enough. Alcestis felt powerless. Of course she had known that

Eurycleia was desperate, even out of her wits. But she had never imagined that she would run from comfort and status – for what?

"If I were a man, I wouldn't rest until I found her!"

Megacles took her hands. They both knew there were many things she would do if she were a man – and many things that though he was a man, he would not.

"I'm sorry, Alcestis. She has shamed us, and Archilochus. And that poor boy. She can do as she wishes, but it's for his uncles to find Melissus before she can do him – and his prospects in Attica – much greater and lasting harm."

Alcestis shook her head. She would not hear it. She did not believe in giving up on anyone or anything that mattered to her.

"I shall never judge her as you do, with no understanding of the case."

"No doubt," he said, and held on to her hands so that she could not withdraw them. "But then you are too generous."

"And I shall never abandon her."

"Let us hope the gods have the same intention. You must leave Eurycleia in their hands, and forget her."

Alcestis pulled away, her freed hands closing into fists at her side.

"And how do I do that?" she wondered, steadying her voice as it began to rise. "Is it in my weaving that I must immerse my mind and spirit, or in considering the provisions for the next drinking party – which I may hear but not see? Perhaps it is the boiling up of flowers for perfume that will absorb me entirely? Should I take longer baths at the fountain?"

"You are a mother, Alcestis."

Megacles breathed slowly and his chest sank, but he was not angry. The rage was all hers. She knew he allowed her to be a different kind of mother, respecting her ideas however unconventional they might be. What could she say? She had children to prepare for Athenian society as it was, not as she believed it should be. She had left Corinna sleeping in the bed they shared. Now the small girl ran to her, hair wild, cheeks flushed and eyes squinting. Alcestis lifted her and stroked the fair strands from her forehead.

"I'm sorry, my sweet, did you wake and find me gone?"

Corinna nodded, too sleepy for words, and pushed her head in against her mother's softness between breasts and shoulder.

"Come," Alcestis told her, and wishing her husband goodnight, carried her daughter back to the women's quarters where they belonged.

Corinna too would be a mother, a nurse, housekeeper, clothes maker, and all too often the arbiter in disputes between slaves. She would marry a man she did not know and be shut away from the rest of the world – except when permitted, once in a while, to attend tragedies in the theatre, or festivals for women only. If she produced too many babies she would die, like most Athenian wives, worn and aged, before she was forty. Alcestis kissed her as she laid her down, and pulled away from the warm arms round her neck. Corinna was asleep already. Easing into the bed beside her, Alcestis wished that she could hope for the same simple peace.

In the slaves' quarters Damastor woke himself with cries. Startling those who slept on either side of him, he earned a kick from one and a push from the other. The darkness was almost complete, but he was used to that. It was the blackness inside the dreams that was hard to breathe through. Not that it was new. But he had been free of it for a while, and tried to forget. He didn't know where he was, or why, when the air thinned and heated around him, pricking and tickling him into gasps of panic. He felt the tightness that trapped his limbs and sealed him in, as if he was in a coffin, buried but living, and all that he could heave from his mouth was noise, bursting from his lungs. No words and no meaning. Nothing. The world was a tomb and he had no mind and no strength to escape it.

"I'll break your jaw," muttered a voice Damastor knew well. "That'll keep your mouth shut."

Theognis was a thug. By day his threats were a habit, unwelcome but easy enough to ignore – and for an eight-year-old, easy enough to dodge. By night they seemed flimsier than the dreams. He was one of the more muscular slaves as well as the fiercest, but one day Damastor would be stronger as well as younger than he.

"Break his nose, Theognis," murmured another slave. Damastor could hear the smile in the voice. "He's much too pretty."

"Quiet!" came a hiss across the bodies. "Leave the boy alone, said Hesiod, his defender when he chose to be. "You too, Damastor," he whispered. "Enough."

Damastor straightened and loosened again. The mattress itched. The smell of feet and night-breath mixed with the dull scent of earth. Sleep now, he told himself. Breathing deeply, he imagined the kiss Corinna had placed on his forehead before bedtime.

Chapter Six

Twelve years later

Corinna had not seen Lysias for a while. His education and military training kept him at the gymnasion, so that in the summer months he was a rare visitor at the farmhouse. The sight of him, his shoulders broader and his legs thicker from exercise, took her by surprise. Her smiled faded into sudden alarm.

"You scare me!" cried Corinna, wincing away from her brother as if from dazzling sun.

"Do I look like a man?" asked Lysias, and grinned boyishly.

Corinna nodded anyway. Nineteen now, he was a soldier in the making. But Damastor, who stood behind him, was older, taller and much more sculpted than Lysias could ever be. Her brother's square chin and asymmetrical nose seemed to have grown sharper edges now that his scalp was severely domed. His hair was thick and dry but little more than stubble and not for stroking.

With its girlish shine, Damastor's hair made her want to touch it. Rising tall above Lysias, he was at his shoulder, slave to master, attending as required. But now that they were no longer children, the light that used to fill his face lay always in shadow. Rules they broke in innocence could no longer be flouted, but for Corinna it felt as if an unwanted wall had blocked out that light and cooled the air between them. She looked back to Lysias. Yes, he seemed like a man – a short one of a kind never seen on any vase or modelled for a podium.

"That's why you scare me," she said. Then she saw his concern. "I could never fear you! Not like I fear our father and his friends."

Many times she had heard them at their drinking parties, cheering and jeering as they flicked wine dregs into a bowl as if it were a sport for princes.

"Maybe it's time that frightens me," she said. "It races faster than Damastor."

"No one races faster than Damastor!"

Lysias gave Damastor's back a light slap of approval. But he knew what his sister meant. A kind of dread troubled him at night when he dreamed of her, offered up for a kind of sacrifice.

"Don't worry," Lysias told her. He took both her hands. "It's not going to happen. We won't allow it to happen."

Corinna smiled faintly, grateful that he knew and she did not have to explain. Sixteen soon, she was of an age to be married and taken away. Even her mother did not want to talk about it, dismissing the subject as if it were no likelier than snow in July. But Corinna knew the time would come. Lysias would most likely have to fight on the frontiers of Attica. She would be a bride with a husband she had seen once at a distance – or heard, in the wine-loud crowd at a symposium. And Damastor? Wouldn't a dog have more freedom, more joy?

"Why do we have to grow up?" she asked. "There's no choice and we can't resist."

Her brother only told her there were questions no one could answer but the gods. She glanced at Damastor a moment, wishing she could challenge him to hear her, to see, to be his own self again. But he stood still, his eyes on the olive trees, or the sky they interrupted, as if such matters were no concern of his. He was the slave porter now. It struck Corinna that his duties meant he would most likely know her future husband better than she did. Would his life ever change? After all, he had nowhere to go – no battles to fight, no marriage to submit to. Porter now, chief slave before long, perhaps? Attached to the household for as long as her father chose to keep him – and why would he sell his best slave?

"What do you think, Damastor? Should we resist growing up?" asked Lysias, genial and encouraging.

"But we grow stronger," said Damastor, looking down to some weeds, half-choked by dust and buckling, "as well as faster."

"You do!" said Lysias.

Corinna was glad to smile, but sorry that Damastor did not.

"Minds grow too," he told Lysias quietly, his focus unchanged, and allowing the breeze to blow his hair across his eyes. "Yours must be crammed with wisdom by now."

"Stuffed like a cow's bladder!" joked Lysias.

Excited by the exchange even though she felt apart from it, Corinna grimaced at the thought of the tasty treat filled with blood and fat, a dish her father relished.

"You're disgusting!" she cried. "I'll have to ask Damastor to pin you to the floor and silence you."

"Maybe I can no longer be pinned," boasted Lysias, stiffening his neck and stretching folded arms. He beckoned Damastor. "Come! We'll see."

Damastor hesitated. Corinna frowned, anxiously glancing back towards the house.

"Theognis!" she hissed. "He'd love to see Damastor flogged."

"He's not a god!" scoffed Lysias. "He can't see through walls and trees."

They were too old for horseplay now. The punishment for striking a free man was a fine of a hundred drachma – if the blow came from another citizen. If a slave did the striking the fine was paid in blood. But Lysias was in earnest.

"I order you to test me out! I haven't been wrestling daily for nothing. Come!"

"No, Damastor!" protested an anxious Corinna.

"No slave can be beaten for following his master's orders!" cried Lysias.

As Corinna sighed, Damastor sprang. In a scuffing, dusty moment punctured by grunts and gasps, he tripped and trapped Lysias, a long arm under his chin.

"Unfair!" Lysias claimed breathlessly, and straightened as Damastor released him. "I wasn't ready!"

Corinna saw her brother's shoulders fall, as if he was dispirited, before he managed a rueful smile for Damastor.

"I'd best get back to the gymnasion," he said, "and find out how you did that."

"Please don't," said Corinna. "Not yet."

"Better still," continued Lysias, "why don't you do it again and break my back! Then I can forget all this and become an orator, admired for the power of my speeches instead of my biceps."

He remembered when Damastor had carried a rod with him, in the days when he accompanied him to school, charged with the duty of beating him should he deserve punishment. It seemed long ago. Grinning, he reminded them both.

"You should have taken your chance to break my bones when I argued with my teacher," he added.

"You told me he was wrong."

Damastor remembered too. Once he'd pretended to use the stick, around the corner of the school, and the two of them had faked the sounds, Lysias groaning and gasping and whimpering while Damastor beat laundry and tried not to laugh. Old days, and old ways.

"But Lysias is never wrong!" cried Corinna.

Seeing that Corinna was exchanging faces with her brother, exaggerated faces like the masks the actors wore in the theatre, Damastor allowed himself to watch her a moment, unseen. The sun dappled her, turned her skin to barley and honey. Her green eyes smiled at Lysias as they fought, word for word, jeer for jeer.

Damastor pictured the drunks who left the house less steadily than they arrived, sometimes stained and always discoloured, their chitons creased and their breath acid. Important men, all of them, and many of them looking for a wife. Which of them would spurn a girl so fair, who could sing like a bird? Damastor would rather fight the Spartans than stay to see such a marriage. And if he were not a slave...

I love you, Corinna, he told her silently as she turned to him, the words slow and deep inside him, like a speech to a great crowd. He felt their weight before their leafy lightness. Thin words, too slight, and airy. *If you were mine I wouldn't trap you in a cage. I'd let you fly.*

From the entrance to the house someone was waving to them, telling them to come.

"Father?" mouthed Corinna.

Without a word, Damastor ran off to the side of the house, leaving Lysias and Corinna to walk inside together. Corinna linked her arm with his.

"I have a plan for Damastor," he told her as they watched the long legs kick dust ahead of them. "But it's not one our father will approve."

The night that followed brought Corinna sweat and shivers. Again the same dream dragged her from sleep with wide eyes. She lay afraid in the darkness, as still as she could, so as not to wake Alcestis. If she had not been to the temple of Artemis two years earlier... If she had not been sent through the woods to find the oracle, she would be spared this face. Beautiful and crazed, it shook her with its whiteness, like the moon returning, again and again. But this moon face had eyes as dark as a storm. With saliva beading her mouth, the oracle chanted, eyes upward, entranced, while scented smoke thickened and clung. No truth could come from such bitterness swirling. Those few words lifted, tossed high as the curling grey. Lost in shapeless mouthing, they had drifted beyond reach, disappeared like the smoke in rain.

Death in life. No air to breathe. No love, no life. Could there be a crueller prophecy? Another had followed, like the other side of a spinning coin. But it could not erase the first. Corinna had never told Alcestis. She lay stiff, and pictured a different face, a face she used to love when she rode on the shoulders that supported it. What plan could her brother have, and would it exclude her?

Chapter Seven

October

Alcestis pushed her tongue hard against her teeth but the word broke out anyway.

"No," she told her husband.

Megacles took a deep breath and more wine. He silenced the slave with the lyre; the last string plucked a squawk. Lysias sat straight, his fingers gripping the ram's head cup.

"Father…"

"This is not your concern."

Alcestis stood. "It is," she said. "It is the duty of every man of intellect and spirit to examine such a custom, and to consider whether it must be so, or should be so."

"I will not debate this, Alcestis. I see no alternative – unless you would see her become a priestess or a courtesan."

"Sir," said Lysias, "might I meet the citizen you intend for her, talk with him, and judge for myself?"

"I don't think Antiphon would take kindly to being examined like a slave at the market!"

As if on cue, a slave girl poured more wine. Alcestis shook her head and covered her cup. Megacles admired her still; she did not doubt his faithfulness. But he did not respect her enough to balance her judgement against Attica's, and feel its weight. Corinna would be betrothed and she must help her to accept it as she herself had done.

"Then let him *be* kindly, if he is capable of kindness. Let him understand that he is to receive a gift beyond price. Make him grateful."

Alcestis let her eyes plead. Megacles met her gaze, and she saw his shoulders loosen. She knew he was sorry, but it made no difference. She rose, and stood where the light from the brazier might golden her. He reached out and laid his hand briefly on a fold of her peplos. Alcestis lifted her head high and let her damp eyes shine. There was little more she could do.

Among the epheboi Lysias was renowned for his wits. He could hold an audience in his power, and make them laugh or cheer. But here, in his father's house, argument felt as hopeless as outracing Damastor. Unless...

"Sir," he began, "I was very young when my mother's father died. I did not have the pleasure of learning at his feet. But I know he was a man of honour and wisdom – such good judgement, in fact, that from among those fine Athenians who would have been proud to marry her, he chose for her a husband worthy of her cleverness and grace."

Lysias bowed to his father. Alcestis turned, smiling as graciously as she could.

"Indeed he did, and I thanked him, every day and every night."

Megacles nodded. "I too." He sat up straight, as if the chair had become a throne. "And I shall follow his example. Of course! What else? Antiphon's an old fish! He can take his money to a different stall! Corinna shall have a husband worthy of her."

"If such a man exists in Athens," murmured Alcestis, and accepted more wine. She had never been so proud of her son.

The next morning Damastor found himself alone with Lysias, summoned to help him dress.

"I have to leave, Damastor, but I need you to promise two things."

Damastor allowed himself no frown; his eyebrows did not rise. He simply waited.

"Keep running. Run as often as you can as fast as you can, until I return. Eat to run. Sleep as well as you can. Like me, you must consider yourself in training."

"If those are your instructions."

"They are! Come, Damastor, do you think Theognis listens behind the door? These are my wishes. I want you to help me overturn society! Expose the falsehoods and the illusions! I want to make you famous for ever!"

Damastor had known Lysias enthuse before, about ideas he could not follow, but the last time there had been no stubble to shave from that square chin of his and his singing voice had been as high as Corinna's, though not as sweet. He nodded.

"As you wish."

"I do, and you will be glad."

Lysias hesitated now. The other request was a waste of breath. What could a slave do, after all?

Damastor knelt to fasten his sandals.

"Will you poison any suitor who is not fit to marry my sister?"

Damastor looked up, forgetting his mask. His mouth widened with his eyes.

"Or rather, would you find a way to shame him with too much wine, drug him with herbs to make him stupid, spread malicious rumours at the market..." Lysias laughed. "Or get word to me, so that I can ride back and run him through with my sword!"

"Is Corinna to marry?"

Damastor heard the stupidity of his question, and its temerity.

"She's of age," Lysias told him. "Of course she's too good for any man I know."

"She's too good for anyone."

In his own voice, quiet as it was, low as footsteps, Damastor heard everything: anger, horror, love. Surely Lysias heard it too? In that moment Damastor did not care. He would have liked to shout it from the highest hill in Attica, so that it carried across the Aegean: *Corinna is too good for anyone. Including me. Especially me.*

Megacles was on his way. They heard his stride as, hungry, he issued orders.

"You may go," Lysias told him.

Damastor bowed and left.

Weeks later, it was Damastor's duty as slave porter to admit those invited to the betrothal feast – held in honour of Thasos, who would be Corinna's husband in the month of Gamelion. Megacles had spared no expense. Word had reached the slave quarters that Thasos was a rich man, much travelled and learned too. He was so unexceptional in appearance that Damastor did not realise at first that the feast was for him, until the floral crown was placed on his head.

Neither tall nor short, neither muscular nor feeble, Thasos had crinkled hair flecked with grey, and a pale complexion, so that dressed in white his skin faded into the twilight. His voice was quiet and his manners modest.

It seemed to Damastor, called on to serve wine late into the celebrations, that the guest of honour was the most sober man in the room. Everyone knew the old story of the husband-to-be who had danced drunkenly on his head, kicking his legs wide enough to reveal a lack of undergarments – and forfeit his bride. Damastor could not imagine any way of making Thasos ridiculous. There was ribald talk, some of it loud, but it did not come from him. There was tuneless singing, but Thasos only watched and listened.

Megacles was not as sober as his future son-in-law, and made a short speech acclaiming the virtue of Corinna. Slurred and repetitive, excessive and foolish, it brought a blush to Damastor's cheeks. The words were a formula. They did not speak of Corinna, her loveliness and music, her healing ways and delight in colour, in flowers and birds, or her small, quick hands and throaty laughter. Damastor hoped she slept.

Pouring wine for every man in turn, Damastor reached Thasos. As he stopped to pour, the guest of honour flicked a quick dismissive hand at the jug, knocking it just enough to tip a splash of wine onto the floor. The spray that spotted the fabric draped around Thasos was fine, and the evening lamplight thin, so that Damastor could hardly see the stains. But Thasos growled low in his throat, his neck muscles tightening. His hand gripped Damastor's wrist, jagged fingernails stabbing briefly. Then he let go, and turned to an oblivious Megacles with an attentive ear for his story.

Damastor stepped back, shaken, his eyes on the neck as it loosened again, leaning in receptively. The fingers that had pressed so sharply were slow now, thumb stroking forefinger in a gentle circle. *Never*, determined Damastor, as he pressed like a robber against the wall. *Not while I live.*

In the bed they shared in the women's quarters Alcestis and Corinna were awake, their hands joined. Corinna lay on her back, eyes upward in darkness. The sounds from the andron were not unfamiliar, but never before had she thought she heard her name amidst the babble.

"How long?"

"January. Gamelion is the favoured month for weddings."

Corinna knew all this. It was sacred to Hera, the marriage guardian. She did not want to talk of it, but she needed to be sure.

"But first I must go to his house, to prepare?" she whispered. "You will be with me?"

Alcestis placed another hand on top of Corinna's, which still felt cold. She closed the cool space between them.

"I shall. His mother too. She may want to wait for a full moon. Then you will dedicate to Artemis all your childish toys. I shall dress and veil you. We will return to your father's torchlit aula, where the guests will be waiting."

"And my husband too."

Corinna heard her own voice, steady as a vow, as if the birds in the net had stopped fluttering.

"And his groomsman. Your father will offer a lamb. And after the feast I will hand you to your husband, who will lead you to his chariot. Between the two men you will ride away, with torches and song, to your husband's house."

There was more. Confetti, and the presentation of a quince, the symbol of fertility, for her to eat before the guests at the threshold of her new home. Another feast, in a perfumed and flower-hung marriage chamber, before the doors shut behind the departing couple. Corinna pictured the doors, ever closing but never meeting, always an opening for light to chink through. As if she might pull them apart and run between them!

Thasos. To Corinna the name meant nothing. She did not want to guess a face, or imagine a touch. Any touch but Damastor's. Corinna's eyes widened and stung in the darkness.

Damastor was a slave who should never, by Athenian custom, have been a friend. Her mother's unconventional ideas could come to nothing in the end, nothing but this ceremony in which she was to be honoured, and helpless.

Corinna rolled onto her side, her hand withdrawn. There was no comfort. She was alone now, for the first time. Alcestis could not permit herself tears. She dared make no assurances that would betray her daughter's trust. Was Thasos the fine and honourable man Megacles claimed, or believed, him to be? If he fathered more children than Corinna could wish, and slept with others as and when he chose, he would be no less honourable in society's eyes than most married men. If he ignored his young wife, her thoughts and feelings, that was his right as a citizen. Such behaviour would be considered reasonable and to be expected and Corinna must smile serenely, and ask for nothing more.

"You will be a good mother, my sweet," she told her, and turned away to the wall, appalled.

It had come to this! Education, imagination, questioning – even her attempts at rebellion! Lysias had done his best; Megacles had good intentions. But Athens had defeated them all.

"I will," said Corinna, and closing her eyes as if they might shut out the sounds of celebration, wished her mother goodnight.

Lysias was at the baths. In the steam room he sat, counting the time before the plunge pool. The other men spaced around him sat equally oily, red and silent, their secrets intact as his own. He should have been there at his father's house, could have been, had he wanted to be. The gashed leg he'd acquired in training made riding painful but not impossible. Stiff and swollen around a wound not yet sealed by new skin, it spared him further swordplay as well as his sister's betrothal feast. He was glad of it. But he could not allow it to hold him back, not now that he was surprising himself and everyone else with his horsemanship. He might not have the strongest arm, the best aim, the fastest legs or the heart for war, but on the back of a fine animal he had the stature he was used to lacking. A little more practice and he might no longer shame his father.

Lysias heard in his head the vows of the epheboi. The fourth was his favourite, for he was determined to leave his fatherland better and greater, as far as he was able. It was the fifth that had troubled him, and sounded like a lie on the air. He would obey the magistrates and the laws, for now, and defend them against those who sought to destroy them. But there were laws he would change too, if he could. And the gods, who had been his witnesses, would understand. They would applaud him.

Many of the guests in the andron were slumped or sleeping as night became morning. Pausanius, a distant cousin to Megacles, became unintelligible. Damastor was obliged to lean over him to make out the words squeezed from a mouth hanging loose and dribbling, but eventually he established which wine was required and poured it into a cup that tilted and at one point swayed. Noticing a silver ring with a ram's head on a thick finger, he thought that this man's horns would be incapable of butting. His richly dressed fingers could barely grip.

Later, when most began to stir themselves to leave with the aid of slaves, it became clear that Pausanius could not move. The wine he had demanded had tipped from an angled cup and splashed his solid calf. Overweight, he looked flushed, his head hanging back, his mouth so wide open that Damastor expected a snore to rattle him awake. His slave approached ready to offer support, but could not rouse him. Dumbly he raised a hand.

Something in his face brought Theognis rushing. Damastor saw the alarm sound in his face as he beckoned him over. Hesiod moved in close to Megacles, who stumbled up and roared, beating his chest with a fist. Pausanius was dead. The wooden handle of a small knife rested against his back, its blade disappearing into wool. A second dark red stain, growing steadily on the plaster beneath the couch, was not wine. Megacles was suddenly lucid.

"He's warm. The blood is fresh."

Movement stilled. Damastor and the other household slaves stood awaiting orders. Among the guests who remained the words were repeated until silence followed. Thasos stood and scanned the room, lifted one arm and pointed his forefinger.

"Bind him!" he said, and his own attending slaves grabbed Damastor by the arms.

Chapter Eight

Alcestis and Corinna woke to a household scratchy with silence and scrubbing. The lingering smell of sweat and wine made Corinna nauseous. Feeling a sense of secrecy in the busy quietness, they asked questions, but met only dumbness and denial. Then late in the morning Corinna overheard Damastor's name whispered by slave girls sweeping in a corner. She called them to her, and asked them to repeat whatever news they might have, but they claimed to know nothing.

"He is in trouble. Where is he? I must know."

The girls, who were not much older than herself, only kept their eyes down to the floor as if still searching for dirt to clear away.

"You have been told not to tell me? Is that it? I am not to know?"

One of them nodded. When she asked if her father was at home, they all agreed that he was not. Then someone fetched an unwashed and sleep-tousled girl who had danced at the andron the night before. Corinna remembered a story Lysias had told her about this particular slave, Theognis and a bucket. The girl was curved like a woman now and looked as if she'd overturn such a bucket on his head if he ever tried again.

"Please," said Corinna, who could not remember her name. "Tell me."

The slave girl stood for a moment as if she hadn't heard. Then she wiped her hands down her hips.

"There was a murder," she said, "and a robbery. Damastor didn't do it."

Corinna clasped her hands. The girl's eyes were pleading.

"No," said Corinna, squeezing. "No."

Damastor had heard of guilty men hung by their hands, wrists and feet outside the city walls and left to die. There were stories of huge winged birds pecking at living flesh. He knew too of slaves who had been whipped and branded for lesser crimes than the murder of a rich citizen. In the cell where he awaited trial, mice scrabbled in straw. Damastor was glad of them – of their living and moving, for sounds that were not hostile.

The other men chained in the same space he took for slaves like him. One, no more than a boy, only sat facing the wall in a corner, furthest from the light that broke through under the door. At times his silence shook into whimpers. He seemed unable to hear Damastor and unwilling to look in his direction.

Another, who seemed drunk, roused himself now and then to glare at him and accuse him of staring. Then he would shout angrily for food, for wine, for the magistrate, and when his demands went unanswered, kick the wall and floor.

"Do you confess to the murder of Pausanius?"

Damastor heard it again, from the mouth of his master, as if each word slapped hard across the jaw, the mouth, the cheek. It had felt as if Megacles had never seen him before.

"I do not. I did not kill him."

Each word of the denial felt to Damastor so much like insolence, and an insult to a citizen's memory, that he half-expected to be struck. Megacles only looked agitated and weary. There were details to add, such as Damastor could recall them, and Megacles had simply heard, offering no indication on his face, his voice or silence, whether he believed or doubted him. The words felt fragile and useless, as if they changed nothing and left no trace.

It had been many hours since his master had left him, saying little and promising nothing. Not that Damastor blamed him for that. The dead man was, after all, his kinsman, a member of his phratria. No, Damastor knew very well where to lay the blame. But he could not imagine why a stranger like Thasos should make such an accusation against him. There was no explanation – unless he could read his mind, his heart and soul.

Damastor's speed was no use to him now. He needed power, money, knowledge of the law, and the intellect to use it. He needed Lysias, and Lysias was far away, learning to fight the kind of battle for which he had no aptitude or stomach. And did Corinna know? Or would Alcestis protect her, and pretend? Did Alcestis know that he loved her daughter, more than Thasos could ever love?

The kicking prisoner beat his feet on the floor so that Damastor breathed in the dust through the blackness, and coughed. The man spluttered. Damastor heard the hiss of his spit.

"I confess!" yelled the man. "Execute me now!"

The door rattled menacingly. The man pulled himself up straight, pushing his back against the wall, as if he thought he might burrow into it.

"I jest!" he shouted. "It's a joke. I'm innocent."

He retched and vomited, then fell silent and still. Damastor could smell the pungent puddle not far from where he sat. The boy in the corner had begun to cry. Pulling himself up suddenly, the drunk leaned as close to Damastor as he could and when he whispered, his breath was bitter with vomit.

"I'll kill the jury if you pay me, one by one, with my bare hands!"

His knuckles hard and his teeth clenched, he gripped the air as if to choke it. Then he spluttered, as if such hands were around his own neck. Damastor had little faith in the jury. He knew Thasos would direct them which way to vote with their pebbles. He would be convicted, and die, and never see Corinna again.

He could not have explained why he felt an emptiness that was almost calm. Perhaps some part of him had not understood that, unlike most of the events that had happened around him, this concerned him. It was only the cold that made him shiver, and he hoped no one would think him afraid.

The boy murmured, "Mother, Mother, Mother. . ." like a curse between his teeth until the drunk kicked him from behind.

Alcestis stared at Corinna.

"Wall-diggers! You are sure?"

"Yes, Mother, I'm sure! Listen!" Like the fountain she could hear staggering in wind outside, Corinna's words came in a rush. "I told the slave girls who danced last night to check, and they found the place where the thieves dug through the bricks, with wind whistling through."

Starting to explain the location of the crumbled entry point, she stopped, arms gesturing helplessly.

"I sent for Hesiod but I didn't know whether he would come at my calling. It isn't the first time wall-diggers have taken their opportunity by night, during a feast, remember? When I was small, I heard Father..."

"I remember."

Alcestis felt no surprise that the house had been robbed again. The bricks were of sun-dried mud and crumbled easily enough. At a feast most of the household slaves were needed in the andron, leaving the house virtually unguarded, and packed with rich men. It was not the information that astounded her, but the determination of the daughter who brought it, who had summoned a slave to do her bidding. Corinna wanted to pull at her mother's hands like an infant. There was no time for reflection or wonderings.

"Mother, don't you see? It must have been one of the robbers who killed Pausanius," continued Corinna.

Alcestis saw Hesiod waiting in the shadow behind the doorway. He was her husband's oldest slave and had served at their marriage. She gestured to him, as if to show confidence as well as faith. Betraying no astonishment at the behaviour of these women who had strayed so far beyond custom and expectations, he stepped inside.

The cell door was stiff and juddered open. The light arced in, blinding, and the boy yelped like a dog that had been beaten. The man with the kick, who had been sleeping, jerked awake as two guards stepped inside. Damastor knew they came for him. Whatever crimes the others had committed, he doubted whether they matched the murder of a rich citizen. Justice must be done, and quickly, in a case like his. He had learned as much from accompanying Lysias to school. Standing, he watched their hands as they unfastened him, his mind focusing numbly on fingers and sounds. He had slept little and prepared himself to die, just as he would prepare himself to run – with determination to do it well.

Megacles was waiting to accompany him. Head low, Damastor knew better than to look above the hem of his master's chiton. Nor did he expect Megacles to pay him any more attention than a bucket where he must urinate.

"Do you maintain your innocence?" he heard him ask, and nodded, remembering not to hold up his head as he answered.

"I do."

"And you saw nothing?"

Damastor shook his head. It had been a noisy night, long and wearing. His clearest memory was the hands of Thasos around his wrist. The image had obsessed him, and obsessed him still. Hands that must never touch Corinna! As if he had just awoken, he breathed the sharpness of the wintry air and let it fill his lungs. It was not how he died that mattered, or whether he died at all. What must be won was her freedom, from slavery to such a man. If only he had the brain of Lysias. If only, like Lysias, he had the education to defend himself and a birthright to respect.

Through the agora they walked, a chill wind nipping at ankles, and dark puddles reflecting a sky Damastor did not raise his eyes to see. His feet, along with the others, seemed to stumble into a shared step that filled his head with its beat as they crossed the square. Damastor did not care to see any of it, and left the ten great statues to rise above him, glimpsing only two huge but unidentified noble feet, cool and damp and smeared by a passing bird.

A few more wind-beaten steps and they had arrived in the People's Court. The jurors were waiting, gathered like a chain around an ankle. The space they circled was smaller than Damastor had imagined. They would be close enough to see him shiver. He saw the white stones piled ready to be taken, one by one, and placed. Innocent or guilty. Simple as that.

Thasos entered, with two other guests from the feast, and sat to one side. Damastor stood straighter still. His chest must not sink. His neck must hold firm. Hunger growing sharper now, he remembered to lift his head above others. He felt the strength in his calves. He was breathing as slowly and deeply as he could when he registered movement, voices, a stirring.

Megacles stepped outside. There was among the jurors something like a breeze through long grass. He remembered that while there must be no interruptions during the trial, murmuring was permitted. But this grew thick and bubbled like lentils in a pan. He could not hear the words outside, but there was a note within the sound, and a rhythm too, that he knew as well as a song learned long ago. Lysias was here!

As they waited, he felt the glare of Thasos attempt to spike him through like boar's flesh on a knife. Though he dared not allow the jurors to see a smile, Damastor hoped the eyes that looked ahead might shine a message above the head of his accuser. *Never. Do you hear me?*

When Megacles stepped back inside, Lysias was by his side. Damastor noticed his limp, and the weight that had gathered around his middle. Surely this was the finest youth in Athens!

It seemed, however, that an ephebos was not yet a citizen and, however clever, might not address the court directly. This did not prevent Lysias having much to address to his father's ear. Megacles looked troubled; Lysias did not. A herald read the charge of murder. The water clock allowed three hours to argue guilt. Thasos rose.

"We are here to try a slave. Three hours will not be necessary. The case is a simple one."

There was murmuring. Lysias leaned in to his father, who stood too.

"Our purpose is, in fact, to seek justice. I am sure Thasos will agree."

He bowed. Megacles was attempting an easy charm, and Thasos received it without hostility. But betrothals did not generally follow such a pattern! Whatever the verdict, could this marriage proceed? Damastor wished he could look to Lysias, meet his eyes and take from them a sign, sending in return his gratitude. But slaves did not look young masters in the eye. Staring instead at the water clock, it was a message he was attempting to send soul to soul and without trace when Thasos stepped up to an elevated wooden stage.

At the first lie Damastor lifted a thumb. The second, a forefinger. Soon the fingers of one hand were splayed at his side. He listened to one lie after another: that he had carried the knife to peel fruit, when in truth he had only poured wine. That he had been rebuked by Pausanius for knocking his elbow, and leered back defiantly. That just before the body was discovered, he had leaned over Pausanius as if to hear his instructions, while discreetly placing the knife in his back. That he'd had ample opportunity to remove the ram's head ring from the dead man's finger. The other guests, both of whom had by that late hour been incapable of noticing had Zeus himself arrived on a cloud, merely corroborated each lie.

Damastor wished Megacles had been sharper that night. But he would never know how many more lies might have been told in the remainder of the three hours had there not been a knock and an interruption. Voices, some as low as hisses, met in a hurried exchange and Megacles and Lysias left the court room. Damastor was aware of the shape that was Thasos lowered slowly to sit.

The water clock continued to drip time unchecked. The jurors' silence began to splinter into mutterings. Damastor kept his eyes on the water, and heard in his head the strings of the lyre plucked by gentle fingers. No thought. No hope. No fear.

When Megacles returned he wore a ring Damastor recognised – not from the dead man, but from the hand that had stroked his head when he was small. The healing ring of Alcestis flashed on the little finger of her husband's left hand when he raised his arm in a bid to address the court. Inside the chest he held tight, Damastor felt something like the melting, caving warmth that swelled and sank when he glimpsed Corinna through an arch or doorway.

"I am informed that wall-diggers broke into my house during the betrothal feast." Megacles paused to allow the jurors to assimilate the information.

Damastor began to assimilate it himself.

"My most trusted slave, who has served me faithfully all my life, informs me that this ring…" Megacles held it up, like a small open mouth, and turned it as he continued. "This ring, with a ram's head in silver, was bought yesterday by a jeweller rather too trusting for his own good."

Damastor slackened like unweighted weaving. The muscles and will that had kept him tall and straight seemed lost to an outward breath. Lysias returned to the room and spoke to his father in a whisper – but in view of the level of noise among the jury, he might have shouted in secrecy.

"Furthermore," said Megacles, "since the jeweller noticed blood in the fingernails of the man from whom he bought this ring, I suggest that the charge of murder against the slave Damastor be revoked at once. He leaves this court with his good character upheld."

When Megacles rode home in his chariot, with Lysias sitting beside him, Damastor ran alongside. As he raced he counted in his head each white pebble as he pictured it placed on a pile mounding high, and breathed out to the rhythm of his bare feet landing, stride by stride: "Innocent!"

At the house he was spared further duties for the day. Megacles left him with Lysias a few moments before he called his son to heel.

"Don't thank me, Damastor," Lysias began. "It was the women. My mother and my sister." He grinned. "They always did dote on you. Thank the gods for a handsome face, eh? Not a prayer I'll ever need to offer!"

He hurried at the sound of his father calling his name. Damastor felt the need to lean against a wall and breathe as if he had not breathed all day.

Corinna.

Chapter Nine

Waking next morning, Damastor had never been so grateful for his mattress in the slaves' quarters. He remembered no dreams. But the day that preceded the night felt no more than a vague imagining. As slave master, Hesiod had risen first. He beckoned Damastor over.

"I fear your duties must be more menial from now on."

Damastor stared back, puzzled.

"Think, Damastor," continued Hesiod. "As slave porter you would have the duty of greeting and escorting Thasos, and however rarely he visits…"

"But surely now…?"

"Betrothed is betrothed, it seems."

"But he…"

Damastor held back the word. Many of the slaves were glad to see him safe, but some would advance themselves by whatever means necessary. It was Hesiod who had taught him discretion, and warned against trust.

"Thasos has apologised to the master," said Hesiod, "who is, as you know, more forgiving than most."

Damastor felt his fingers tighten. He spread them loose before they formed a fist. Hesiod glanced around him, scanning faces. Tilting his head closer, Hesiod spoke again, this time in a voice that was low and deliberate.

"That which you wish most can never be. You know it. Seal it off, like everything else you feel. You must bury it before others catch sight of it too."

Then he straightened and moved away.

"The master wants you to attend the horses instead of the guests," he called, barely turning his head.

Damastor nodded.

"Now," added Hesiod.

In spite of her relief, Corinna had not slept peacefully. She had heard her parents talking late the night before, and felt the tension in Alcestis when she joined her in bed. As her mother adjusted her position again and again, all limbs restless, Corinna had not asked questions. Pretending sleep, she had told herself that Damastor was safe and for that she must be thankful.

Waking now, she remembered at once that he was alive. Nothing else could have the least importance any more. She would marry Thasos as she must, and be the best of wives and mothers, if Hera would only give her peace from all the false notes jarring and clashing in her head.

It was not hard to imagine the conversation between her parents that had disturbed her late into the darkness. Alcestis had asked Megacles to break with Thasos, on the grounds of the false accusation against his slave. Megacles had refused. And until the world changed, there was nothing her mother, or anyone else, could do.

A slave dressed Corinna's hair. It was habit only that held the mirror; she had no care for pins, nets, ribbons or scarves. But the shawl over her shoulders was a comfort against the winter morning. She was close enough to the window to see outside, but did not count on sunshine that day or the next. The lyre rested against a wall. The slave, seeing her look to it, brought it for her. But the music felt less like birdsong and more like rain, and her voice, slow to lift, had the sound of mourning. Corinna stopped. Her mother was calling. She held out the lyre, rose and embraced her, puzzled by the brightness in her face.

"Come with me to the river, Corinna."

She must have shown surprise. Lysias slept still but she had wanted to see him. Alcestis touched her mouth with one finger. Corinna looked behind her, wondering whether she had come from her father. She nodded, and slipped her bare feet into sandals.

As Lysias limped outside some time later, breath short, he could not resist a secret smile. His father had been less difficult than he'd expected. Surprised, yes, by a request he could not have predicted, but pleased too, and perhaps relieved. Ten months from now and his plan, which used to seem both theoretical and outrageous, could succeed so gloriously that history would record it. And the future would take a different turn.

He eased his leg into a smoother rhythm and told himself it was healing well, well enough to follow through. Now to find Damastor, and begin.

Not many men looked tall even beside his father's best mare. Lysias wondered that a slave's diet had done nothing to stunt his growth. He was thin, of course, as runners must be, and he knew how to endure.

Seeing him approach, or perhaps hearing him first as the injured leg dragged, Damastor looked up from his grooming, working arms that were long and bare. Lysias was glad of his cloak, and supposed slaves learned to ignore the winter cold.

"Damastor," he said, "I hope you slept well."

"I did. I thank you. Do you require your horse?"

"I shall, but not yet. Please continue. We can talk as you work."

Damastor did not fully conceal his surprise, and hesitated a moment before continuing to brush. Lysias greeted his own horse, whose reply was short but shrill. The mare stood still and passive, as if she enjoyed her grooming, unfamiliar though the groom might be.

"She trusts you," said Lysias, and "so do I."

Damastor was unsure how to reply. He could trust Lysias, if he allowed himself to do anything so foolish, as much as a slave could trust any noble Athenian. As much as he dared. It was not his place to consider his own feelings about anything, least of all the master's son. Or daughter. And he must discipline himself to dismiss...

"We can talk freely, Damastor. You may drop that guard of yours. There is no one to hear."

Lysias guessed he alarmed Damastor. The grin that used to make him smile as a boy might not be enough, but he grinned anyway.

"I have been speaking with my father, and extracted from him permission. Approval. I mentioned to you some time ago that I had a plan. I cannot yet explain it fully, but it concerns you, and will take you away from your duties here."

Pausing as he brushed the mare's creamy neck, Damastor could not help looking up. Though he glanced briefly at Lysias he was picturing someone else. He did not see her every day, though he looked for her whenever he might, but he knew she was there, and would be there the next day, and the next. He knew she would be sleeping not far away as he slept, thinking of her.

Lysias rebuked himself. He despaired of teachers who ambled along via the longest, most winding route. It was time to make his point.

"I want you to be my personal slave and come back with me to the gymnasion. Help me train. Get me fit. I am good with horses but I need more stamina, to improve my balance, and develop more strength in my arms and legs. I need people to believe that I can enter the Olympiad next summer as a charioteer."

Lysias heard himself and laughed suddenly. It sounded ridiculous and Damastor must think so, privately, however composed he might be as he focused on the mare. In fact, Damastor was still thinking of Corinna, until the words settled and gathered meaning. He looked startled.

"You mean to compete in the Games?"

Lysias only smiled, as if it were some kind of joke or game. He could not blame Damastor for his surprise.

"I could not find a better trainer. And then you will accompany me to the Olympiad."

In Damastor's head he recognised a mere idea, not a place he might go or a spectacle he might see. The Olympic Games. The fastest, strongest. A statue of Zeus, reported to be tall as seven men, on the spot struck by a thunderbolt hurled from Mount Olympus. Crowds beyond anything the theatre could attract. And glory for the greatest.

"I should be honoured to be there."

"You shall be! It is decided."

Damastor looked at the short legs and hands that remained big and clumsy. He had heard of transformations worked by the magic of gods. Could this be a trick of the kind played in stories, when they took on human form? Or did Lysias, serious-minded, opinionated and intellectual, interested only in the speed of a man's thinking and the strength of his character, really mean to devote ten months of preparation to a chariot race?

Perhaps Lysias guessed his thoughts. For a moment he looked almost sheepish. Then his grin widened.

"You doubt me, but humour me too, Damastor, I beg you."

Damastor bowed. There was nothing to say and no point in thinking. He would only serve as ordered, even if that service took him far from everything he had known and the girl he loved. She would be married soon and taken by a different kind of chariot to the house of Thasos. He would never see her. So it made no difference whether Lysias had lost his senses. He might as well follow him to Hades.

"When..." he began, and did not finish.

"Tomorrow. I shall rest today, and amuse my mother and sister – if they can be amused. My father has business in the city."

Lysias knew Damastor hid more than he could imagine. It struck him that no master, however proud and dignified, was as guarded with a slave as a slave must be, for his own protection, with his master.

"He thinks highly of you, as highly as ever."

Brushing still, Damastor received this in silence. The mare was ready for the finest of riders.

"And when we are together, away from here," Lysias told him, "we can be friends again, as we used to be."

At one glance of a reply he felt shamed. Such nonsense. What must Damastor think of him? What would he think if he knew his real intentions? Yet he meant it, wholeheartedly, if heart dictated anything.

"I wish it might be," he added. "I should be very glad."

Damastor did not answer.

"You will not mind being dragged away from all this?"

Lysias had not considered that it might be home. Might there be among the slaves someone he would miss? That girl with the buckets, who danced now like a wave?

"I am glad to serve you."

Lysias admired the mare. Then he left Damastor with her, murmuring something into one ear that did not sound like words. Walking away, and hearing again the proposal he had made, Lysias grinned to himself. It could work. It was audacious to the point of insanity – but that was the beauty and the point. Damastor would play his part, little though he suspected what that might be. It was his responsibility to make sure he did not fail him. Wondering what possessed him to smile, Lysias reminded himself that now he had chosen it, that responsibility must be taken with all the seriousness of an oath. There was no blood, no statue of any god, no offerings, no vow. But it felt sealed at last.

At the river the wind pressed cloth hard against skin. A recent shower had muddied the banks; the sky above was pale, but streaked with copper and grey. Corinna sat on a rock, her hair straying out from under her hood and spreading itself across her cheek. Her mother stood at the water's edge, directing proceedings while the slaves rubbed the swollen cloth. Then she turned, and with a balance that did not falter, she climbed back across the stones to Corinna.

"I wanted to talk to you," she told her, "without walls."

Corinna nodded. She had felt recently a powerful dread of walls, and how they could close in.

"Before your father went into the city he agreed to prolong the betrothal period. Trials always mean scandal, gossip..." Alcestis gestured behind her to the river. "Wind on water."

Corinna looked back at the sound of the water rushing and snagging, spraying into white.

"We have more time," Alcestis told her. "And time soon brings more scandal, with fresh winds. Memories scatter. Thasos will wait a year."

Corinna stared dumbly. Not this Gamelion but the next. A year was full of change, of sleep and wakening, birth and death. What else could time bring? For a moment, smiling her thanks, she felt a surge that rose, only to fall again. Alcestis embraced her. A shock of sun gathered round them like a cloak, stroking skin.

"It's all I can give you," said her mother, "and I had to fight for it, with every tool I know how to use."

The sun was gone. Over Corinna's shoulder Alcestis saw the slaves bent over the clothes as if to flog them. Ankle-deep, one waded further, the edge of her tunic darkening like the sky. Alcestis remembered Eurycleia carried out of the water by another, more mannish slave who could not speak. So much time had passed, and it had never brought her back.

"It's not much of a victory," she murmured in her daughter's ear.

But Corinna felt warmed. Perhaps it could be.

Chapter Ten

Lysias led his horse while Corinna sat high above him. He smiled in appreciation of her poise, and she smiled back.

"You like it up there, don't you?"

"Of course. It's the most exciting thing that ever happens to me."

"You're a rider now."

"I hope so."

"Has Damastor been teaching you?" he joked, but she didn't laugh.

"And risk a flogging? He daren't come near me these days. He daren't as much as look in my direction."

"I know. It's senseless."

Especially, thought Lysias, since she was to be given to a man who might never feel for her a fraction of the fondness Damastor had shown her as a boy.

"Mother persuaded Father to let me learn."

"She's a persuasive woman."

"Not persuasive enough."

"No," he agreed, "but there's not a mother in Athens who tries harder."

She asked him when he himself would marry. He patted the horse.

"Where would I find another girl as spirited as Mother?" He grinned. "Other than here."

Corinna felt the height and speed the horse gave her like a strength she could borrow. But the ride would come to a halt. He would be gone.

"Will you leave soon? Can't you stay?"

He shook his head. "We leave tomorrow. I'm taking Damastor."

Lysias stopped; the horse stopped. She sat, feeling suddenly stranded.

"Damastor!"

"I need him," Lysias told her.

"He's needed here!"

"He's utterly wasted here, and you know it!"

"How can I know anything?" she cried. "There's not a single thing I understand!"

The horse lifted its head, unsettled. Lysias stroked him. It was many years since they had parried like this, sword on sword. Lysias had not expected it. Corinna began to dismount. As she swung her legs down in a movement that was a great deal more rushed and less elegant than their father would have wished, he held the horse still, but saw that Corinna was the one with a mind to run away. Her eyes were full of something he could not have named. She walked away.

"You must trust me, sister, for I mean to help him," he called behind her. "It will be – I hope it will be – for the best."

Not for me! Corinna did not answer. While Lysias called for Damastor to take the horse, she only walked on, surprised by the tears that tightened her cheeks in the wind.

Corinna did not rise for supper, or breakfast next morning. Alcestis told Lysias she was not in danger, but sick at heart.

"The marriage?"

"Perhaps the life."

Alcestis reassured him that Corinna had lain peacefully beside her in the night, with no sign of a fever. Her skin was cool. She refused to eat, but hunger would prevail before long. Lysias need not be anxious. She did not report Corinna's claim that Lysias was abandoning her. In truth Alcestis was anxious herself. Her daughter's spirits had never been so low. But there was no reason for Lysias to stay.

She held his hands and wished him well, hoping she concealed her disappointment that racing horses seemed for the moment to be his greatest aspiration. It was not what she had hoped for when he astounded listeners as a boy. Alcestis watched him ride away with Damastor tactfully behind. In her bed, Corinna saw nothing but thickly drawn darkness as her eyes squeezed shut.

Some hours later that day, Alcestis was ready to give up on tempting Corinna to eat, after the scent of freshly-baked honey cakes had failed, when Hesiod appeared. He brought the news that someone was asking to see her. Alcestis frowned.

"To see me?"

"The slave porter sent word, mistress."

"I am expecting no one but my husband," Alcestis told him.

As a woman, she might as well be forbidden to entertain guests. And she did not like Theognis, the slave porter. She had advised Megacles not to promote him.

"Will you accompany me, Hesiod?"

"I understand it is some kind of priestess," said Hesiod, taking his place at her shoulder.

"Then she is a fish out of water," muttered Alcestis.

As they approached the front of the house they heard a scuffle of beats and sweeps. Theognis appeared to be jabbing a staff at a figure half his weight. If this was a guest, it was one who seemed determined to dodge her way inside and might have slipped through any available cracks. A guest who trailed robes heavy with dirt and rain, and carried an acrid stench. It was a smell like rotten fruit and fetid herbs burned black, and reminded Alcestis less of the farm than the cemetery. The woman's hood hung low and obscured her face, but her small, blackened feet danced away from the staff. Nimble, silent and faceless, she ducked and evaded as if used to such a reception. Alcestis reached out in protest. Hesiod snapped at Theognis, who lowered the stick and held it like a spear, assuming the position of a guard at a fort.

"She tried to barge in," muttered Theognis.

The woman pushed back her hood. Hair fell loose and dank across a white forehead. Beneath were large, wide eyes, so fiery that they might hiss with heat like lead in a furnace. So like, but so changed!

"Sister," murmured the woman, hands knitting as she bowed her head.

"Eurycleia?"

At the name her mouth opened wide. Laughing, she revealed a curve of dark-stained teeth that had shrunk or subsided. It was a rattle of a laugh, drier than it used to be, but Alcestis knew it well. As they embraced her bones jutted, snap-thin, like the bird remains that in a fortune teller's hands might tell the future's story. Alcestis did not believe in soothsaying, in tricks or spells or curses. But she had long believed that one day there would be a moment not unlike this, yet not the same.

"Praise Hera!" she murmured, the taste of smoke and unwashed flesh filling her mouth as she drew close.

"All praise to Aphrodite!" cried Eurycleia, and looking over her shoulder, hearing without seeing, Alcestis felt her own face stretch around a smile, reshaped and new. It was her. She was alive. They would be together again. She pulled away, but reached out both hands.

"Come."

They walked past the two slaves and into the house. Alcestis led Eurycleia through to the garden where she might bathe in the fountain. Stripped of her robes, which Alcestis handed over to slaves to be burnt, she was skeletal. Her flesh was marked with dirt and sores, emerging ghostly pale as she scrubbed under the spray, while a thin tune lifted from her thrown-back head. She sang like Corinna. Except that this song seemed to have sprung from a tomb and leaked away as it died, back into the earth. Alcestis saw her shiver, and hurried to wrap her round.

"Thank you."

"What took you so long? So many years! Where have you been, and how…?"

She stopped. How had she lived? How had that living led her into such degradation? How had she survived so long? There would be time for questions. Alcestis linked an arm in hers and led her inside, where she sat her by the brazier and sent for a peplos and cloak.

Sitting as close to the heat as she could, Eurycleia allowed her body to loosen, her shoulders to fall and her neck to lift as she stopped shaking. The clothes arrived and Alcestis helped her dress. She smoothed her, and wiped the wet hair that bedraggled down, but Eurycleia warned away a slave who moved to dry it. Alcestis took the cloth and rubbed it herself, steam rising above the brazier like the faint wisp of another song. Her cousin's lips, which had hung torn and purple, filled with red as she warmed.

The two women did not speak while Alcestis styled the fair hair, and showed her in a mirror how it piled and curled.

From behind and above, Alcestis saw the shock of recognition in the reflection. Eurycleia was no longer beautiful, but she belonged again to the old self they had known together.

Then, as she turned away from the mirror's image, her hands wrestled, pulled and tore at each other, clasping only to tug apart. The silence was punctuated by the slap and suck of flesh. It was the sound that recalled the funeral, and images Alcestis had tried to forget. The face of a boy, burned from inside, skin breaking dry. Was he dead? Dared she name him? Alcestis crossed to the brazier and stopped the hands that fought, resting them in her own.

"There," she murmured. "You are warm, you are safe, and now you shall eat."

Corinna feigned sleep when her mother came to announce both guest and food. Alcestis stroked her daughter's hair as she whispered. She raised her voice to a low and steady murmur but Corinna was breathing deeply and stirred only to turn away. Unconvinced, Alcestis withdrew and watched Eurycleia eat with the passion of a wolf with a carcase.

Corinna opened her eyes and stared at the window, watching the movement of branches across the light. Since she did not rise for the rest of the day, the first time she saw Eurycleia was through a haze of twilight. From her bed she heard a sound that had drifted like smoke through her dreams – a nasal whine that opened out into a wail and seemed to spiral and swirl like notes that would not rest in place. Not music, but yearning. Or pain. Frightened, Corinna crept closer to the sound. Safely hidden in darkness unlit by lamps, she looked out. Crisscrossed by the branches was the familiar yellow of her mother's peplos, swaying like a flower in a storm. As she moved closer she saw the figure inside it, arms spread and reaching, snatching, twisting, as if calling down the moon. It was not her mother.

This time there was no temple, no scented smoke and no offering, but Corinna had seen this woman before. She drew in a fearful breath, for she had heard this voice, speaking a prayer that danced and mourned and cried out in triumph as well as agony. Corinna had been a girl, away from home, receiving from the mouth of a priestess a message, a prophecy. A promise.

"One eye, one hand, one lip, one foot," she had told her then, touching each in turn, showering her with breath bitter as ash. "One of two, paired and never parted. Blessed of the gods is she who will be loved by he who loves her, and walk with him always. Eros and Psyche kiss."

Perfect happiness. The cruellest lie of all, and Corinna had hated her for it. She would be sacrificed. There would be no love and no happiness.

And now the priestess who had betrayed and mocked her was here, staying in her house, mad as lightning. Writhing, she flicked fingers like flame towards the window, and Corinna felt the eyes draw her own. Outside the priestess danced on, but as she moved she held Corinna in her gaze. Corinna closed her eyes and tried to fill the darkness with the faces of her brother and Damastor, and hear their voices. As if they were there, only steps away, in the house with her.

Waking, she felt as if something had been lost. Instead she found the strange figure in her mother's yellow, almost motionless now behind Alcestis, like and unlike, a bad portrait. The woman followed as her mother took her arm, leading her to eat.

"This is my beloved sister, Eurycleia," Alcestis told her, "back from the dead. A gift from the gods."

Through the lamplight Corinna saw her smile as a cold hand stroked her cheek like cobweb.

Chapter Eleven

Approaching the house as darkness thickened, Megacles determined that the move from farm to town was long overdue. The weather would get no warmer and the journey back from business in the city no quicker or easier. Mud had slowed the wheels of the chariot and he was hungry as well as tired. He could tell at first glance that Theognis had something to tell him, something he would not like. Not that he liked Theognis, but he was ambitious, and that made him conscientious. One word from Megacles and he would take on Hesiod's duties as eagerly a horse snatching an apple from a palm. But for now he was slave porter, and rather less dignified than Damastor. He was clearly anxious to pass on news that Megacles was sure would not be good.

"There's been a visitor? A guest? Still here?"

Theognis nodded and bowed.

"Where?" demanded Megacles.

Not, from the direction of the glance, where a guest should be. Alcestis had her own ideas and he was sure they were largely enlightened, if looked at from the right perspective, but she had never pushed them so far as to entertain in his absence. Not, at any rate, to his knowledge...

As Megacles made his way towards the women's quarters he heard a laugh that was not his wife's, and not Corinna's either, though he had not heard that for quite some time. The laugh itself was not quite stable, but he could not believe it belonged to a woman so disgraced that no respectable household would admit her.

"Alcestis!"

She did not hurry. He found her rising from a chair, her expression far from guilty. As he strode into the room he felt a presence behind him. He turned only long enough to see his fears justified.

"I was so glad to welcome Eurycleia," began his wife.

"I cannot share your feelings."

Eurycleia stepped forward. Megacles saw she had changed. Not so beautiful now, and the eyes more unnerving than ever.

"Do not cast me out."

Eurycleia spoke slowly and so quietly that he almost wondered whether he had misheard, or imagined. But the message carried by her eyes was a warning, not an appeal.

"Will you put a curse on me?" he challenged her. "You will not shame my wife the way you shamed your husband."

"I beg you," began Alcestis, "let me pour you wine. Be seated, and Eurycleia will explain. She has been a holy priestess at the temple of Aphrodite, and revered as a teller of truth. As you see, she is not strong and has no possessions but the clothes that burn outside."

"The truth is that she has no dignity or self-control, and no conception of the duty a wife owes to a husband, in death as in life."

Alcestis raised her eyes to his, held steady, and poured wine. She held out a cup, a favourite painted with an eye on each side. Megacles knocked it to the floor. Startled, Alcestis flinched, but made no sound as wine spilt, rusty on the dry earth floor.

Megacles felt sorry, and ashamed. He looked down at the broken cup, at one flat eye cracked through, the brown paint flaking away. But four brighter eyes fixed on him. Two of them felt deep enough to pierce through armour, but all of them were judging him. What could he do but walk away?

The walk was a march, and the house was not big enough to contain it, breaking his stride with its corners. With all its side rooms no bigger than cells and lit only by open doors, it felt oppressive as he remembered his business in the agora with all its space, and pulse of life. In the andron, empty of guests, he opened the shutters to feel the air again, and breathe it greedily. The hillside hummed. He drank the night like wine. Turning, he heard the soft tread of a slave girl, carrying a jug. Megacles beckoned her. He rested on the nearest couch before he remembered the knife in the back that had rested on it, and the blood below. He gripped the jug tightly, because everything else felt stained and broken.

The disturbance began with a thud that sounded no heavier than the split of the painted eye. But the rhythm grew steadier, louder, sharper. He heard the beat of wood on flesh and bone, and cries forced out without words. Making his way onto the balcony he looked down on two figures knotted like wrestlers some distance away from the entrance, where they merged with bushes and trees.

The stick he had heard lay snapped. All the noise that was not the scuffling of feet came from one throat, one mouth and nose, grunting and cursing, as Theognis kicked and twisted. The other, who might have been his twin in height and build, fought back in silence.

"Stop, Theognis!" yelled Megacles. "Bring him here."

But who was it? Who dared to fight the slave porter at the entrance itself, and what had he done to earn such a beating? Had he the strength to break the staff in two?

Theognis had stopped after another lunge. He picked up the halves of the stick and held them up like evidence. The other figure hung back, straightened, shoulders steady, with no sign of exhaustion or shortage of breath.

"Who are you?" shouted Megacles.

Theognis answered instead. "A vagrant, Master. I found him trying to sleep back there."

He reached to grab the man in question, who dodged, slipping past to step in front of him and look up to the balcony. The face, shadowy as it was, looked wide, the cheekbones strong. In it Megacles saw no trace of anger or fear.

"Wait!"

He hurried out, taking a flaming torch from Hesiod, who had brought two others with him. By its light he could see a scar that ridged on one cheek, tugging it higher, and a bruise that darkened the forehead. Megacles lowered the torch like an artist brushing colour. It revealed lines that moonlight had not.

"I know this slave," he said. "Hesiod, see that she is fed and washed and has a space to sleep inside." He would have liked to see his slave porter's face. "The gods play tricks from time to time," he told him, "and make fools of us all."

Megacles watched the slave they called Chorus walk beside Hesiod, her head above his, no longer alert for combat but loose and trusting.

"She's insolent," said Theognis, smarting. "I told her to move and she would not stir. She refused to answer me. Then when I raised my staff she grabbed it like a dog."

"She's deaf and dumb."

Theognis looked sullen, almost resentful. Megacles would like to sell him for a good price. For now, he left him to consider his mistake and recover from the injury to his pride. Megacles returned to his wine, weary and uneasy. Nothing was as it should be, and it wasn't the fault of a surly slave. Or any slave at all.

Alcestis left Eurycleia sleeping in a chair, covered with a cloak. It was a comfort to see her dark eyes closed, to find her lost not to frenzy but peace. She had been assured by Hesiod that Chorus was settled in the slaves' quarters. It was late and Alcestis was exhausted. Now she might slip in beside Corinna and try to rest, at least. But all through her marriage Alcestis had been determined not to retire, after disagreement with her husband, without a gesture, a touch, a word that recovered the tenderness. It was a substitute for understanding and sometimes she felt its feebleness. But it held. It had always held, until now.

If he did not come to her, the rules made it hard for her to take the steps, to venture into his territory. But she had broken the rules before. She must show him that she remained loyal. Patience, endurance, strength and generosity. They were not so different from submission, but for a wife they were necessary.

She found him alone and sleepy, surrounded in the andron by decoration and emptiness. Feeling the cold, she wrapped her shawl tightly. He did not stir as she approached and she thought at first that his eyes were closed. She placed a hand on the curve of his head, down the back of his neck. He sat up, his eyes challenging.

"Eurycleia must go," he told her. "That mute brute of a slave may be in her power but you are not. You are my wife. This is my house. I will not have her here."

"Megacles, she is half-starved."

"She chose hunger."

"She does not choose. She is out of her wits."

"But I am not, and I choose. She goes."

"My dear, have pity," she murmured. "Eurycleia is sick. She needs me. She has no one else."

She reached out her hand to his but he did not take it.

"She had a son!" said Megacles. "What has she done with that wretch of a boy she dragged away with her?"

"She has not said. I too am anxious for him. But let me care for her and I am sure…"

Megacles sighed. She was too good and he was no match for her.

"Stay with her, then, if you must. I shall go to the city. I will take Theognis and leave you Hesiod. That will please them both. Cure her if you can – if she's not a sorceress who'll bewitch you while you sleep. Take care of yourself, and Corinna too."

What was he saying? He did not fear a homeless madwoman without a drachma of her own. He served at the altar and hailed the name of Zeus, but he did not believe in any power stronger than democracy and money, law and reputation.

"I will be back in the spring – and find one of them gone. Either Eurycleia herself, or her madness."

He offered a smile. It was cool but Alcestis was glad of it.

"Thank you," she said, and kissed his hand.

Chapter Twelve

The end of winter

Corinna looked up from the strings of the lyre to find the slave called Chorus in the doorway, as if she might be listening – or imagining, perhaps, what music might be. Corinna smiled at the thought. What would she picture, without sound? Sunlight dazzling? Breeze whisking flowers into dance? A cave that led on and deep into darkness? Forest branches reaching high?

Sometimes Chorus worked beside her, slicing through fish, spinning wool, picking olives or chopping herbs. They were at ease together in the silence. Chorus neither smiled nor frowned, but had a stillness that calmed Corinna when she would like to sleep for ever, or hide, or only play and sing but never stop to live. Sometimes it was easier to communicate with a nod, or a finger, a grimace or clap, than to try to make sense of the loose threads that did not mesh, the holes and snags and patterns out of line that were woven with wild abandon by her mistress Eurycleia when she spoke.

"Still kissing," she would say, from time to time, her eyes bright, as if it were a code, a shared secret between them.

Once she wrote Eros and Psyche with a wine-dipped finger on the plaster floor, and a heart between them.

"Perfect love."

But could she really remember Corinna, or her own prophecy, when she often seemed to have forgotten where in the world she was, or her status in that world? There were times when she ordered Corinna as if she were a slave, or stroked the mannish head of Chorus as if she were not, or called Alcestis her mother and begged her not to die.

Not long ago the slave girl with the curves had come to Alcestis to complain about Eurycleia. It seemed that late the night before, she had insisted that they slipped outside to dance in the winter fields. Then, overhearing sounds from a house not many miles away, she had dragged the girl in through a back entrance to dance some more, this time for the men at a feast. The girl had been embarrassed even before the guests jeered. Eurycleia had danced in a way that was unseemly for a woman of her age.

"She kept her eyes closed and stroked her own hair."

They had been ejected. Then there had been the time when Eurycleia had burned and inhaled the pungent scent of some Egyptian leaves she bought in the market. Her eyes had reddened and her eyeballs tilted and slipped as if in oil. Alcestis had poured water over her cousin's head when a lock of hair caught fire.

She sang, with the voice of a spirit who would soothe Zeus himself. She sang, with the open jaws of a wolf with a thorn in its paw. She played knucklebones for hours, her focus tight and low. She sat on grass with her parasol when there was not even the wintriest of suns in the sky.

After supper she liked at times to invite the household, including the slaves, to an impromptu performance without a theatre, in which she pretended to hold up a series of masks created by her own changes of face, and delivered speeches about love, birth and death, gods and revenge. And once she spun naked in rain until she fainted into mud.

But Corinna had not forgotten the time she had woken to find her with a knife, cutting her own arm and holding a chous below to catch the blood. Would she have drunk it, if Alcestis had not come, and quietly swapped it for wine while Eurycleia closed her eyes and waved her arms, as if to clear smoke that was not there?

In the two months since she arrived, Eurycleia had given a variety of answers to the important questions. Sometimes they sounded plausible. More often they contradicted each other or made no sense.

"Where is Melissus now?"

"The birds pecked out his heart."

Or, another day: "Where is Melissus, sister?"

"Melissus lives on. You see him in the weasel, the one with the blackest eye. You see him in the quail listening in the doorway, head-a-tilt, hopping away with wings that can't fly."

Corinna tried too: "What happened to Melissus?"

"His skin cracked open and out poured blood, hot and steaming, a tide to carry him away."

And once, when Eurycleia seemed distant, as if she barely knew her, Alcestis took the voice of a stranger, as if in a trial, and asked, "Where is your son?"

The answer came like a reflex: "Ask Chorus." Then she laughed.

"Is Melissus alive?" persisted Alcestis.

"Drowned." Eurycleia paused, and clicked her tongue. "Stolen when the sky was black. Lost to a fever that licked and spat and burned him away."

Another day she had a different story: "Trapped high in the branches of the golden tree, waiting for the wind to drop him in my palms, when he's ripe and shiny and his flesh is sweet."

When Corinna tried to mime these narratives for Chorus, so that she might shake her head or nod it, the slave became rockier than the hillside and more wooden than the forest. She neither denied nor corroborated. One afternoon when her mistress wept and said, "I poisoned him," she only kept on scrubbing the floor, more vigorously than ever.

But without her father or brother to laugh her suspicions away, Corinna was sometimes afraid. Lysias had sent one written message, delivered by a metic for a fee. *Training is harsher than the weather but I grow tough as a tree – and move a little faster. Sing sweetly, sister, and may Athene keep you golden.*

No word of Damastor, but she pictured him anyway, running up hills ahead of sheep and goats, overtaking barrel-chested riders, and racing out from the shadow of an eagle above.

Thasos sent her a gift from Egypt: a perfume pot shaped like a strange and ugly animal that was not a man and had a tail. Corinna did not like its mouth, set in a grin, or its big bottom lumping out like a handle.

"Baboon," said Eurycleia, pulling a grin in return, and letting her arms hang with a swing. She uttered a horrifying screech while baring her teeth.

Megacles also arranged for a doctor, young and earnest, to visit and report on what he found. Eurycleia tried to remove her clothes and whisper in his ear before pretending to be asleep – so successfully that she fooled everyone but Chorus, who held out a hand to lift her up from the bed the moment the medical man had gone.

As winter lingered frostily on the hillside, Eurycleia took to gazing out in long, focused silence, narrowing her eyes at each colour that moved. But she also insisted, late in the evening when others were tired, on telling stories. They filled her with excitement that extended to her fingertips as she stretched, linked, pushed out and pulled in with her hands.

A Cyclops ate so many sheep that it choked and spat out blood-red wool. Nymphs sang to the fishes until they were too sleepy to swim and sank like stones to the ocean floor. Athena tricked a man into marrying a goat that butted him out of the house each night. The stories had no beginning and sometimes their listeners feared they would have no end.

One night when Alcestis was obliged to leave a board game to mediate in a dispute between two slaves, Eurycleia pushed the board off the edge of the low table.

"Have I told you the story of the infant in the pot?"

"No," admitted Corinna, "but it sounds a cruel story."

"The gods are crueller. They decide. Stones in a pile. He lives. He dies."

Eurycleia stared at Chorus and put her forefinger to her lips. "Hushhhh, sweet, don't tell."

She cradled an imaginary baby in her arms, and as she dandled it Corinna saw a tear that clung and shone. Chorus stepped up and reached out for the invisible infant. Then she handed it to Corinna, who received it with care. Eurycleia hugged herself, rocked back and forth and lowered her head close to her lap, where it hung just for a few seconds before she lifted it and smiled.

"Lead, Aphrodite," she said, "and I will follow."

Rising she walked away. Chorus watched her a moment, then loped after her.

As an observer, Damastor enjoyed the mock sea battles in the flooded stadium. Though there were no waves to swell over the hulls of the narrow ships, the ploughing and turning and pattern of the oars soon carved the flat surface into mounds and gullies. The sound of shouting, of swords clashing, and water slapping wood, shook and rattled the air.

Exercising under a covered portico, Damastor looked down and tried to make out his master, hoping he might remain on deck a little longer this time than the last. Lysias laughed at each failure and shrugged off humiliation, but as a swimmer he floundered and gasped. Damastor hoped someone else would rescue him if he threatened to drown in his absence.

As a slave he had helped create the flood and would later speed the drainage. He swept the walkways and around the baths. But he was also there, whenever time allowed, to coach Lysias in all the skills he must refine before the Olympiad. They ran, lifted, boxed, wrestled and rode – and threw and caught when they must – though Lysias could not have dropped more balls had they been made of lava from an erupting volcano.

And while Lysias listened avidly to the visiting philosophers who gave open-air lectures under the porticos, Damastor ran. It had become a joke between them: how far and how high could he go, and still be back by the end of the last answer to the final question – normally asked by Lysias himself as Damastor headed towards the stadium with the raised hand of the questioner in his sights.

Damastor breathed out. He stood a moment, reached down for the log that he must lift above his head in one swift, straight-armed move, and saw Lysias leap across from one deck to another, lurching but keeping his footing. Damastor smiled. His master would be in high spirits tonight. Thinking of the brother's stumpy awkwardness and the sister's natural grace, he felt more miles from Corinna than any map would show. He thrust upward, the log high, and as he raised and lowered his arms, his thigh muscles tightening and loosening again, he heard her name like a silent charm, repeated with the rhythm of the lifts, lodged in his head breath after breath. One word, one thought. He could not name her aloud in the hearing of her brother.

They talked, the two of them, more than the rules of the household had allowed on the farm. Or rather, Lysias talked, often with animation and laughter, and more about childhood than the future as he shaped it. Damastor listened, nodded, even smiled, and answered as simply as he might. It seemed to him the present could never be shared like the furthest past.

"What is the first thing you remember, Damastor?"

So Lysias had asked, early that morning, when they ran before breakfast. Damastor did not know. Perhaps the earth flying beneath his feet? The air in his lungs? No. That was choice, not memory. Not beatings, though he had bent for a few, sealed against tears by a mouth that learned to harden like baked terracotta. Memories, he recalled, of friendship that could not be.

"A cartful of quails," he said, smiling.

Lysias laughed. "Yes! My backside always in the dirt. And holding back a goat for you to race it!"

"I won."

"Oh, you always won."

In fact, as they talked, one runner had moved ahead of the other in spite of his efforts to remain alongside. Lysias was becoming breathless already. There was something in the glances they exchanged – something between them as they ran, that Damastor guessed neither would have wished to express. *What can I win now, Lysias? Not even a voice of my own.*

"You must remember more! Even you were not born running. How can we trust experience when so much is lost?"

What have you ever lost, Lysias? What can you know about losing everything you never had?

The pace was too slow. Lysias needed waking up. Less talk, more urgency. Damastor challenged him to keep up.

"Have you ever kissed a girl, Damastor?" Lysias called as he fell behind.

Damastor drew further ahead, ignoring the rain that threaded the cool air.

So clever and yet you do not understand what the penalty might be – or how vigorously Theognis might impose it. Not that I would ever want to kiss any girl but one.

Lysias stumbled, hobbled and willed himself on. If this was a drill, twenty soldiers could march in the space between them now!

"Neither have I. No girl would let me near," he called. "Like you! Let me catch you!"

"You can't say that to the charioteer in front in the hippodrome!"

Damastor could imagine it, some of it – the crowds, the beating hooves of the horses, the track that looped around, lap after lap, the whips flailing and the wheels spinning. The hard part was picturing Lysias still upright, still commanding, and not left behind in a haze of heat and dust.

Now, as he finished with his lifts, he decided he needed a heavier log tomorrow. The sea battle seemed to be over for several epheboi bobbing in water, but Lysias was not among them.

Damastor would have liked the gods to liven proceedings with a three-headed monster. It might snap its jaws close to the necks of those who held their heads too high to see him, who brushed past him without an apology, or pointed out dirt when he was sweeping as if he spread it at their feet out of spite. Were slaves and citizens so different under their skin? Could a doctor tell them apart by examining what was left when time had stripped bones and outstripped memory? It was a question for Lysias to ask the next philosopher who stopped by. But not for him. *Damastor, you insolent dog, you forget who you are!*

"But who am I?" he breathed white into the cold air, and ran towards the water where Lysias was obliged to splash and wade before he could claim victory – only to trip within reach of land.

As the mornings grew lighter and the afternoons milder Alcestis began to expect her husband's return. The dark months had brought a number of changes that might surprise him.

Corinna sang again, played the lyre more liltingly than ever, and slept at night. The baboon pot had disappeared and Alcestis did not ask where she had hidden it, since in its absence the name of Thasos was never mentioned. With Megacles at the town house, the betrothed suitor did not call, and whenever Corinna's spirits paled, Alcestis began stories of Lysias that she knew his sister loved to hear. She coaxed Corinna to join in, correct details and add her own accounts of events that only the children had shared.   Listening to such stories, Eurycleia sometimes laughed aloud, but if instead she sat bright and silent with tears, Corinna took her hand, no longer afraid.

The other change that Megacles would notice, perhaps at once, was in Eurycleia herself. Perhaps the doctor's herbs had worked a healing no one could explain. Perhaps nourishment, rest and care had been enough to calm the storm. Her skin had softened and her eyes lightened, as if the heat in them had cooled. Fewer bones protruded and as Alcestis told her, a gust of angry wind was much less likely now to blow her to Piraeus harbour. She was rarely lucid, but she no longer removed her clothes, drugged herself with strange potions or sang like a wolf by night.

The household was oddly peaceful. It had become so quiet and productive, in fact, that Alcestis hoped her husband might step inside and feel it, like the steam on wash days. Then he might greet her, the way Eurycleia had begun to greet Chorus on waking, with a kiss.

As she paused in her weaving on an afternoon lit by sudden sun, Alcestis noticed Eurycleia unravelling the wool she had carded, wrapping it around her wrist and watching her fingers as if in a trance. Looking up from the lyre, Corinna held the strings still with the palm of her hand. She glanced outside to where a distant Chorus carried branches for chopping.

"Melissus left me," said Eurycleia, and her mouth hung open, her forehead creased, as if until now she had not understood. "Sweet revenge for a bitter god."

As Alcestis rose Eurycleia dropped the card. A thin spill of wool trickled slowly to a stop. Corinna reached for a hand that fell loose before she could take it. Alcestis laid her cheek a moment against her cousin's, and feeling no breath, closed the startled eyes. Outside Chorus shook wood from her arms as if it blazed.

The body of Eurycleia was covered in flowers. Together Alcestis and Chorus washed and anointed it while Corinna played the lyre. The dead woman had no family to gather round her; there was no one to invite. Alcestis planned an oration of the elaborate kind that might be expected, wording it fretfully through the night, but next day, as they watched Eurycleia lie untroubled, the silence felt more truthful.

Chorus did most of the digging, allowing Hesiod to take a turn only while she took short rests. Since her cousin owned nothing that might be buried with her, Alcestis placed her own favourite pot of cosmetics and combs, its lid alive with galloping horses, in the tomb beside her. Then they left an offering of honey cakes and gave praise to Aphrodite, the goddess she loved best.

Returning a few weeks later, Megacles asked few questions.

"Trust me," Alcestis said, and stopped his mouth with a finger. "Let us be at peace now."

His time away had increased his stature in the city and swelled his purse, not least because he had sold Theognis for an excellent price. Eurycleia no longer stood between them. He held his wife and remembered how much he had missed her, how clever she was to manage everything without him, and how proud he was of their fine son, preparing to compete in the greatest Games in the world.

Chapter Thirteen

The start of summer

Usually Lysias felt more at home in the library, where he could exercise his mind, than in any other part of the gymnasion. The air was cooler inside, and the tasks that faced him suited him better. But the heat that browned the grass was a sign he could not ignore. Flesh was sweating. Grasshoppers were as busy as the epheboi, but a good deal quieter at times. The hillside was fiery with flowers opening out in hope of rain. And it all meant the same thing: time was pouring through his fingers like a handful of dust. Soon the rehearsal would make way for the performance in a packed theatre, and he was not sure he knew his lines.

Lysias was sure that even the loyal Damastor privately considered him deluded. Among all those at the gymnasion he knew only two others who might consider themselves ready to register for such a competition.

One was Pheidias. As one of the sophronistae, he was a figure who generated fear among any student whose behaviour might have lacked discipline. He was also a wrestler of some renown and intended to prove that age had not weakened his body or his will to win. The other was an ephebos like himself, known as Boulos, who being small and light was a bareback rider with his eyes on the Olympic hippodrome.

No one, thought Lysias, needed to consult an oracle before declaring both their chances better than his own. In fact, he was afraid that one of the gymnasiarchs might send for him any day and explain to him that his personal disgrace in the chariot race would mean shame for the gymnasion itself, and for Theseus. In spite of Damastor's best efforts to build his strength and stamina, he simply wasn't good enough, and if he was banned from entering the Games, it would all be for nothing. His plan would sink like a ship in a sea battle, the kind that wasn't pretending.

To have come so close, thought Lysias, and to give up, would be more than frustrating. He made a fist in his lap. It must be followed through. He owed it to all those Athenians who were yet unborn, to a new order that would one day replace the old, to his mother and sister. And Damastor. Because Damastor was good enough, and though they had been careful not to flaunt it, there must be those who had noticed, who had begun to guess how good he could be.

Elis was far enough away. They would be two in a crowd. There was a danger, of course, that he would be recognised. But Pheidias was known for poor eyesight, attributed to the efforts of an unusually ferocious opponent to gouge out one eye. And when Boulos saw rather less of Lysias in the hippodrome than he expected, he would assume he had pulled out, having seen sense at last.

Lysias had always known that success would only be possible if they held their nerve. If they believed. If the gods admired their audacity – and saw in Damastor a man who might have stood in for any deity busy elsewhere.

They would leave before anyone could stop them. Tomorrow.

Each day seemed hotter than the last, and Megacles, who swore he had never known heat of such intensity, needed a good deal of fanning. Corinna took a turn as he spread his increasing bulk on a couch that had been carried out into the courtyard.

"It will be cooler in Elis," he told her, when she sighed that racing would be intolerable for Lysias. "It has more rain. The forests and pasture are better there."

Corinna had imagined her brother passing out in the midday sun and being dragged through dust behind his chariot. It was harder to picture Damastor, watching in the hippodrome. Where would he be? Surely slaves would not be allowed seats near the finish.

"Why can't women go to the Games?" she asked.

"Women have their own games. There's a temple to Hera too, although I doubt the statue reaches up to the knees of Zeus! But you'll be married by the end of the year. No married woman can compete."

"Married women can't do anything," she murmured. "I don't suppose they can even sit and watch."

"You suppose correctly! The Games are for men, boys and unmarried girls."

The fan remained mid-air above his head. He looked up before she could protest.

"You, my dear, are not such a girl. You are betrothed. Thasos would not approve. You are aware that the athletes … well, enough said."

He took the fan and waved it quickly as sweat gathered around his chin. Corinna had heard that the competitors would be naked, and might have teased her father for her amusement, but spared him this time.

"Might I go with you, Father? I am sure you would like to cheer Lysias. You must be so proud."

"If I might cheer him, I would indeed be proud." Megacles sighed. "I have business which prevents me. So there is no one, I fear to escort you." He stretched and yawned as Chorus poured him wine. "I understand that women can own horses competing in the hippodrome," he added." You will have to ask Thasos to buy you one."

"If I had a horse fast enough for the Olympics," said Corinna, "I'd ride it myself."

And I wouldn't stop, she thought, *until I found a land where I might be free.* Her father laughed. Then his expression sobered.

"Your mother has encouraged such banter. I myself have indulged you, and I fear recent influences have loosened your tongue in a way that will not be welcomed outside these walls. I would counsel you, Corinna, when you are married to Thasos…"

"Not to speak, think, or suggest by gesture or glance that I have feelings or opinions of my own?"

Megacles had closed his eyes. Now he opened them again; she read the warning in them.

"You understand perfectly," he said.

"Yes, I do."

Corinna felt thwarted. She had much to learn.

Usually it was Damastor's first duty to wake Lysias. So when he found himself shaken from sleep, a hand lightly across his mouth, he was startled. Perplexed rather than alarmed, Damastor saw the haste with which his master gathered together his belongings, rolled them up and slung them across his horse, without a word. Damastor realised he had been woken at dawn not for training but for departure.

Mounting the grey that Megacles had spared for him when they left the farm, he followed Lysias out of the gymnasion as the sun rose, looking back on a stadium so ochre-dry it was in need of a sea battle.

"What has happened?" he asked suddenly, emboldened by thoughts of illness and death and messages from the farm.

They turned onto a grey-white track where two hens scrambled across, fluttering.

"We are going to the Olympiad," said Lysias, "before someone tries to stop me competing."

Damastor said nothing, although he drew alongside, and the horses were eye to eye.

"You think it is not your place," said Lysias, "to ask me why. So I will tell you: because I will make a fool of myself! And now, you will be silent again, because you are tactful but truthful too."

Lysias wondered what life must be like for one obliged to listen to any stupidity, accept and obey. It made him relish the prospect of teaching the stupid a lesson.

"Don't you want to ask me why I'm so set on spectacular public humiliation in an event for which I have no aptitude?"

Damastor hesitated.

"Have you not always believed me, even as a boy, to be someone who values ideas and principles, and would like to expose the errors that underpin our society?"

Damastor nodded. "I have."

"I am! And with your help, Damastor, I hope to do so. Ride on. Ride on. When we stop to rest I will tell you everything."

As he overtook Lysias around a bend in the track, Damastor felt something more exhilarating than the wind and sun.

Alcestis had to explain to Corinna as they prepared supper that she could answer few questions about the Olympic Games.

"They are held every four years, close to the summer solstice when the moon is full. The sacred truce will already have been declared, one month before the Games begin."

"There will be no fighting across the world?"

"The whole Greek world," said Alcestis, who knew enough to suspect that the world might be a great deal bigger than most Greeks imagined. "Three months without killing. It could become a broken habit, missed by no one."

Corinna smiled. She chopped basil, breathing in the scent.

"I don't suppose the gods send messengers to confiscate all swords and spears?"

"It's a little more subtle than that," smiled Alcestis. "The messengers wear crowns of olive leaves. They are sent out from Elis to every corner of the land."

"To announce the truce?"

"And to herald the Games."

Alcestis was touched. Corinna had innocent faith in Lysias, and it was not for a mother to doubt a son's prowess. Remembering the day he had announced his intention to compete, she recalled her disappointment that he should apply his shine – that quick and eager energy that had always helped him to learn, to focus – to such a paltry ambition.

This from her clever boy who had long seen through the vaunting, chest-puffing, oil-and-sweat masculinity that seemed to count for more than heart or intellect! This from the man she had hoped might illuminate for the men of Athens a shared and profound blindness!

But Alcestis had sensed in him a passion that could not be for sport alone. And she remembered too the whisper meant only for her: "I will be the son you deserve."

What could he have meant? Not victory in a chariot race! There must be more, and she must believe it.

She had sent Chorus to find old swaddling bands and infant clothes once worn by Corinna, ready for a slave girl whose belly suggested she might give birth any day. Of course Megacles would be outraged and want the father beaten, but she would point out the advantages of an extra slave he had not had to bid for, and remind him of another who had exceeded expectations. Looking up, Alcestis saw the clothes were found.

"Ah!"

She smiled at Chorus, who was standing in the kitchen doorway with a clay pot in her arms.

"Corinna," she told her daughter, "you must look. You will remember."

Corinna turned to see, and looked back at her mother. Chorus was straight as always, but so stiff through her limbs, her chest and face, that she might have been carved and mounted on a pediment. The muscles in her neck were tensed. Her eyes, fixed full on theirs, communicated something that held her tight.

Chorus looked down at the side of the old pot. There Corinna saw letters, smeared and faint. D A M...

Chorus set the pot down, crouching on her haunches like a child, her balance steady as she traced the letters with a finger. Once again she looked up at Alcestis. Corinna glanced at her mother. She knew Chorus could not read. But there was a message in her eyes and they must understand it.

"What does it mean?" Corinna asked.

She wiped her hands and hurried to take the slave's hands. She looked back to Alcestis, who had not moved.

"Mother, what is it? She is troubled. Something is wrong."

Chorus hurried to the window and pointed to the green mound thick with flowers where her mistress had been buried.

"Eurycleia?" said Corinna.

Turning to Alcestis, stony still but for fingers that fluttered by her side, sealed and spread again, she saw that she at least understood enough. Chorus was hurrying back to crouch again beside the pot. She lifted the lid. Inside were the infant clothes, folded and pale. One after another, she handed them to Corinna until it was empty. Then she reached in and gently lifted out something – nothing – cradling air.

"What is she doing, Mother?" asked Corinna.

Chorus pulled her arms apart and opened them wide, her eyes appealing. Alcestis crossed to face her and nodded firmly. Placing her hands together beside her mouth, she nodded again. Then she cradled her own arms, smiled and lifted up her hands to a height.

"I'm telling her the baby boy in this pot lived and grew tall," she said. She pointed to the hills. "He runs!"

On the spot, in her peplos, Alcestis mimed big-armed speed. For Corinna it felt so ridiculous and shocking she might have laughed but for the heaviness leaden in her throat.

"Damastor," she said.

It was not a question, but she looked again to her mother, and saw that she was crying. Alcestis beat a fist against her own chest.

"Damastor is Eurycleia's son."

Still many miles from Elis, Damastor and Lysias lay like soldiers camping out under blankets, and watched the stars. The night was so black and so silent that Damastor imagined he could hear them, like the song-stitchers he had enjoyed on the streets of Athens because they reminded him of Corinna.

"Damastor," said Lysias, "am I deranged?"

No more than I am, thought Damastor, for sometimes it seemed to him that he was afflicted by love of her, and that it was a kind of madness.

"We can succeed, can't we? You can! It's possible."

Damastor heard him fidgeting, rolling over noisily enough to disturb the owls and frighten the wolves. But he said nothing.

"Come, Damastor, speak to me, for you must be me and I must be you. We must turn the world upside down!"

"Then we will fall off."

"Ha! Not us. Some may fall, if they can't find a footing in the new world, for the land will lie very differently. Not us. We will shape it."

Hearing himself, Lysias laughed, the sound big but brittle in the darkness.

"I didn't know," said Damastor, "that you were a potter."

"It is not a jest or a wager, Damastor, but a quest that I consider sacred in its way, and I will protect you – I will try, with all my wit and will."

"I know."

"But I cannot promise…"

"I know."

"High stakes."

"You mean that punishment…"

"Greater for you than me, I fear. But only if we fail. We must carry the crowd with us to this new world."

Lysias felt in the silence the preposterous daring of it all, and the risk. Damastor could have declared that he had little to live for, once Corinna married Thasos. But it did not feel true. Could he live for stars and sun, and air to fill the chest and keep his feet kicking?

"You will be remembered for ever."

Lysias delivered it like a speech, to give body and sound and brightness of colour to something that by night felt like a dream. And smiling, he believed it, because he thought he felt Damastor smile too.

Damastor closed his eyes but the stars remained.

Chapter Fourteen

Lysias pulled the chiton at the shoulders while Damastor stood like a citizen with a slave to dress him. Lysias tugged and smoothed downwards, then stepped back to look. Still it lacked the length a man of his stature required, exposing more copper-coloured calf than most citizens would choose to reveal. But what calves! They gave him hope when he needed it!

"It will do. You lend it dignity."

He had little money to buy another. Lysias brushed off Damastor's old tunic, a little tight across his own chest. Though it had been worn short enough to allow freedom of movement when running, it fell quite long enough for him.

Damastor felt oddly changed. Was it in the weight of the cloth, or in his head? He was not entirely sure that Lysias had considered the practical detail of the height difference between them, except inasmuch as it would enable them to convince the officials who would register the athletes.

"Do I look like your trainer?" asked Lysias. "Don't answer. The point is that apart from your need of a haircut, which we must address as soon as we can, you look like an athlete. I don't need to warn you to guard your tongue. Just remember, from this moment on, who you are."

Damastor said nothing. An exchange of clothes made no real difference. Of course he was more than willing to play his part, but with the competition still a week ahead, there was more than enough time for discovery and disgrace. He could see Lysias was animated by anxiety and excitement, and perhaps by a deeper fear.

But as he stretched and bent, breathing in the new morning, he allowed himself no feelings at all. For in every respect but one, Damastor had felt so little for so long. It was the way a slave must live, and a discipline as exacting as running. Looking at Lysias he knew that pulling on the tunic of a slave had given him no instant insight. And the world of the Olympiad must be rather different from the real one! But what a man this Lysias was, that he alone among Athenians wanted to learn!

They had bought barley bread the day before. It was hard and chewy, but they washed it down with the last of the wine. The horses drank from the stream bed, where a little earlier the shallow water tugging through reeds had provided a cool bath slithery with fish. A laughing, splashing Lysias had claimed they tickled as they swarmed, and told Damastor to catch them for breakfast. They only flickered like sunlight, hard enough to see and impossible to grab as they slid like oil through his fingers.

"Not far now," said Lysias as they mounted, swapping horses too, since as master he had taken the plump-rumped stallion.

The mare seemed less than pleased by the change.

"Do you feel the arrogance of a citizen who rides an expensive beast and expects men to honour him for it?" Lysias laughed. "Of course you don't! I never have!"

They rode on towards Elis, stopping at the first village where Lysias secured a haircut for his new master, and where Damastor produced a few drachma from an unfamiliar purse to buy wine and feta cheese.

There was no need to ask for directions as they rode on. Eyes ahead, it was the colours they saw first, waving across the valley like trees laden with strange fruit, but the sounds soon followed. The quietness of cicada and sheep, goats and birdsong lay behind them now, for they had company. Soon they rode among the craftsmen and food sellers who drove carts or rode donkeys laden with baskets. And when at last they approached the site, Damastor marvelled at an assault of sound, scents and tastes on the air.

"Little Athens!" cried Lysias, and Damastor nodded.

It was like a waking city. Or, from above, an ant hill breaking open at a kick. Once they reached the valley it no longer seemed little but vast and swelling. In the campsite, bright and billowing with tents fitted between the trees, people were already gathering. There were pavilions too, some of them striped, all firm against wind and fit for leaders in time of war. Here high-ranking visitors would sleep, or perhaps conduct business. But Lysias pointed out that for the grandest with money to pay, there were rooms with solid walls, and roofs that would not stir.

Not far away, animal flesh was roasting and a honey sweetness mingled with herbs as stall holders set up under awnings. Among those arriving first were merchants and horse traders. Someone with a bellow to fill a stadium announced that he had the best of all souvenirs. Damastor was hungry, but he sensed that food must wait.

Behind them they saw a curved white building which Lysias called the Bouleuterion. Lysias pointed; Damastor acknowledged it silently. He had been briefed. Here the registration would take place, with solemn oaths.

To the left rose a wall, enclosing the Altis sacred to Zeus. Lysias encouraged Damastor onto the steps that led inside, for a glimpse of the statues facing the temple. On plinths taller than Damastor they were raised up like gods in a line, some holding shields, others a stone torch. Lysias knew that time must nibble the feet of the heroes long dead and discolour their firm skin. But it was impossible, from the earth, not to feel awed by each of them. Solid with smooth-curved muscle, their strength was towering.

"Past victors," murmured Damastor.

"Their names are carved below," said Lysias.

A yellow butterfly landed on Damastor's shoulder. The warm air felt suddenly still. Lysias pointed to another statue, many times higher than the rest, looking proudly down on the winners with a palm branch in her hand. Her lifting wings, taller than a man, curved up to the sky like cool white flames. Damastor remembered.

"Nike," he said, "the winged daughter of the giant Pallas."

Lysias smiled. "You always were a quick learner," he whispered, recalling secret lessons after school.

But the crowd was thickening. They must act their parts, not just at registration but everywhere they went. He straightened and blanked his face as best he could, consciously dulling his eyes like the empty pupils of the statues. Damastor understood and held his head a little higher, shoulders back. Like the victorious athletes they looked up at the temple of Zeus.

"Magnificent," said Damastor, in a tone that mimicked Megacles.

Lysias controlled his urge to smile. Columns thick and tall as trees supported rosette capitals above. The frieze looked freshly painted, its colours bright, its figures godlike. But Lysias knew that nothing decorating the outside of the temple could compare with the gold and ivory statue inside, of Zeus himself, tall as a tree, with lions at his giant feet.

He had promised Damastor that they would climb the spiral staircase to the upper floor for a closer view. Zeus faced the stadium, which lay ahead, stretching out towards the River Alpheios at the foot of the hills. Damastor and Lysias walked around the corner of the wall and looked over to an olive tree where a ladder rested against the trunk. There was something about the tree – not its girth or height but a sense of stillness and awe around it – that told them this was the sacred olive in the Altis from which a crown would be cut for each victorious athlete.

In a green clearing some wrestlers, not yet victorious but eager to practise, were in a tussle cheered on by a few observers. Encouraged by the thought that he might never have to fight again, Lysias looked up to a hill to dwarf others, the hill of Kronos.

Beneath it was a smaller temple in honour of Hera, and between the two buildings, more statues, more trees, and the great altar of Zeus where a hundred oxen would be sacrificed. Curiosity overwhelmed by impatience, Lysias looked back to the Bouleuterion. There would be a long line to join if they did not take their places in it.

Not they. Damastor. He must do it alone. And Lysias must wait, and hope that the next time he saw him he was not being dragged out again to be beaten. Damastor also saw the queue.

"Wait there, near that red pavilion," he told Lysias, with as much authority as he could manage. "I must register now."

Lysias nodded his head in a quick bow and watched as Damastor strode purposefully to join the line. It was not Damastor's intelligence he doubted, and there was no question that he looked the part. He had enough discretion for three average citizens and would keep a dignified silence among the others in the queue. It was his failure to swagger that put him at risk. He carried with him something else that Lysias found hard to name. Whatever it was, would it be hard to mask?

Damastor soon noticed, as the line moved steadily forward, that whatever took place in the Bouleuterion did not take long. Those who emerged seemed satisfied. Behind him were athletes he suspected were from Sparta, where women were reputed to be fast, strong and worthy of respect. He thought of Corinna and wondered what she would think if she knew.

He imagined her fear on his behalf, but did she think of him at all? Would she have grown taller since he left? Would her hair have lightened under the sun or would she spend more time sitting indoors under a parasol now that she was soon to be a wife? He wished that like a winged messenger of the gods he could send his love as a gift. But the idea of presents arriving from Thasos made him tread firmly as he walked, as if to stamp on them.

Once he stepped inside the white building he found himself looking up again, this time to the statue of Zeus. At the foot of it the oaths must be made. There was a busy hush, but no armed soldiers, and no sign of officials scrutinising suspiciously like buyers at the slave market. But the ten men lined up beside the statue must be the Hellenodikai who organised the Games, one from each of the tribes. Some were old, a couple stout and one bald, but the most striking was grey, his beard not unlike the carved beard of the greatest god, but more of a trickle than a flowing rush. They were there as figureheads overseeing while minor officials discreetly recorded names.

Damastor stepped forward as invited and was asked for his own.

"Lysias of Athens, son of Megacles."

There was no gasp of disbelief. He gave his age when asked, and supplied the information that he intended to enter the sprint. He was told the heats would begin on the first day, after the opening ceremony.

"Do you swear before Zeus that you have trained a full ten months?"

"I swear."

"Do you swear to obey the rules in honour of Zeus, your countrymen and the sacred Olympiad?"

"I swear."

It was not difficult to be solemn. He felt the honour. But the sacredness? He felt something of that in the light that woke him and the darkness that always ended. He felt it in Corinna. But he had never needed words, never explored and analysed them like Lysias. They had never meant as much as sleep and food, as sun and breath. Like all the other words these passed but did not touch. All Damastor had to remember was the bow he had seen others make before him. Then he must turn and leave.

With every stride he imagined a hand heavy on his shoulder, a rough tug at his elbow, or a spear across his path. Alert, he felt not fear but readiness, the kind he had needed to avoid Theognis, to steer a path away from blame and punishment, and keep the skin on his back. He stepped out of the building and scanned the crowd. There was Lysias, his shortness setting him apart, leaning in the shade of a tree.

"No slouching!" Damastor rebuked him, hoping the smile stayed hidden. "Stand up straight."

"There are jugglers," muttered Lysias, trying not to sound like a son attempting to persuade a father, "and acrobats."

"I'm glad to hear it."

It was done without triumph, but it was done.

Chorus stood behind Corinna, the scissors opening and closing again, but only on air. Alcestis nodded permission, but as Chorus began, she looked away. Such a wild idea, thought Alcestis! And wasn't she too old now to play the rebel? But if she was, Corinna was not. She sat, passive as a god on his throne, but a good deal smaller, and when her mother looked back again her shorn head was smaller still, hair lying around her feet. Pale curls formed wispy half moons against the floor.

"My dear," said Alcestis, as Chorus cut the last locks falling to one cheek, exposing a forehead for the mother to kiss. "What would your father say?"

Corinna grimaced, less like a lady than a schoolboy conspirator. She could not resist.

"What would Thasos say?"

Alcestis saw Corinna's mischief fade into something more serious and less amusing. She could not decide whether the daughter before her now looked younger or older.

Chorus touched the earrings that hung, cockleshells suspended from tiny boats. Corinna removed them, clinking them together on her lap where she stroked them fondly. Compelled now, Alcestis watched as the shape of the scalp emerged, a little jagged, and not so different from her first view of it when it pushed its way clear the day she was born. The scissors were only neatening, the slicing complete.

Chorus snipped, stopped, and stepped back. She handed Corinna the mirror. It was not horror, or even surprise, that kept Corinna silent as she studied her own face, but a kind of puzzled fascination. The smile was slow, but satisfied.

"The tunic," she said, pulling up over her head the peplos that generally stuck around the combs and ribbons, caught the curls and disturbed the arrangements piled and pinned so carefully. Alcestis held the chiton worn by Lysias some years ago. With the help of Chorus she fitted it loosely around Corinna, and added a cloak to cover the chest that was narrow but not as flat as it must be.

Corinna loosened, and opened her feet, bending one knee. Chorus breathed through her nose the way she did when she might laugh if she could, or chose. Alcestis shook her head, her smile wide.

"My son."

Chapter Fifteen

When Lysias opened his eyes on the first day of competition he knew at once. The familiar smells of roasting, sweat and sweetness mingled as darkness cleared and his waking brain processed each detail. Sitting up, he shivered, and remembered that although he had spent the night outside the tent like a guard, Damastor was within it, sleeping untroubled by significance, myth and history.

Soon they were beginning the day like any other, with exercises. They found space as far away as possible from the camp site and the stadium, where the trees were thicker but the crowds were thinner. They must focus on preparation and exclude the chaos that built as spectators arrived, while those already camping woke, traded or ate breakfast.

"You are a hungry lion," Lysias told Damastor, "tense and alert, one focus only, and all the power of your frame concentrated in a readiness to strike!"

By the time Damastor had stretched his muscles and practised quick-fire starts, the thousands around them had begun to set and move as one, in a block that seemed sometimes too solid to shift. But it was a crowd in which they must separate. The spectators must compete for the best seats sloped in rows up the hillside. Somewhere as close to the arena as possible, Lysias must find a place to be.

But Damastor must take his place among the competitors, and the judges too, in the procession which would enter the stadium. For the first time both of them would see the judges' box, the track that looped beneath and the line where it would all begin. The sun was not yet high and the dew still glistened as the first seats were filled. By the time the spectators had woven colour through stone, the light had brightened. Thick-spun cloud had stretched thin across deep blue.

Dwarfed by the other coaches, Lysias felt stunted but secure. He would not be noticed. But without tactical repositioning he was in danger of missing the moment, when it came, if it came. As the athletes processed in, he leaned and dodged, using each gap as it formed. But were they athletes or beasts? With an open mouth, Lysias began to realise that in this company Damastor would no longer set himself apart.

Among the wrestlers and throwers lumbered a few brutes distinguishable from the Cyclops only by one extra eye. And they were followed by javelin throwers who stretched lean and narrow as pillars! Where was Damastor? Shrunk and shrivelled! No longer god-like but tender and vulnerable, just asking to be crushed!

But there he was, like Odysseus among the swine! Lysias tied around his wrist the scrap of red cloth he had thought to buy that morning, and waved it as high as he could, but Damastor's eyes were straight ahead. Lysias cheered, like all the rest, but with moderation and control. No need for heart-bursting passion. Not yet.

One of the other trainers looked askance at the judges and muttered that he hoped they would remember their promise before Zeus to be fair in all their decisions. Lysias wondered how disputes would be resolved without fists or weapons and whether any such incidents had ever been recorded in the on-site archives.

As the jockeys formed the tail end of the procession, Lysias spotted Boulos among them and ducked behind the broad shoulders of the man in front, ripping the red from his wrist and bundling it inside his palm. He told himself that even if his fellow-student had glimpsed Damastor, who must now be a hundred paces ahead, he would not have known him, not here, so far out of place. While each competitor stood straight, bathed in sunlight like corn in a field, a trumpet sounded. It was the first of many, for before the athletes could begin their heats, the first competition was to decide the loudest to hold his tune. The cynic beside Lysias pointed out the heralds who would follow, their only instruments their throats and lungs.

"Let's hope their voices are stronger than the rest of them!" the man jeered. "Some of them would drop like stones if you handed them a javelin!"

Lysias lowered his head, and exercised what patience he could manage. He noticed as he gazed around the seats that there was barely a female to be seen. His companion had little respect for those few women he identified.

"So-called priestesses!" he muttered. "They light the candles in the temple – among other duties!"

There were a few unmarried girls with their fathers but Lysias did not imagine for a moment that Megacles would permit Corinna to accompany him. Not that he could have located any individual, male or female, among so many! An elephant might hide! Row after row on all sides, here were enough unarmed people to destroy Athens if they all beat hard enough with their fists!

Corinna and Chorus had not arrived in time to find seats, since five hundred thousand reached the stadium before them. Instead they stood at the back, obliged to endure the heat if they wished to observe the spectacle. Corinna had felt less awe in a temple. It was if she must learn to think and breathe. And all the time her legs were weakening.

Suddenly defeated, she sat on the hard, hot ground. Chorus reached an arm down to help her up but she shook her head. Looking up at stronger, taller legs and big male feet, she felt like a child at a late night symposium. They had been too late to see the procession, but she knew Lysias must be somewhere among the athletes, and wished she were closer, or taller. Chorus would see him, she supposed, but did not know who to look for, any more than she would recognise Damastor, wherever he might be.

Corinna felt exhausted already after the longest journey of her life, and not a little afraid of the people who swelled around her and felt more dangerous than an ocean. She wished they need not wait until the third day for the chariot races in the hippodrome, but now that they were here, she would enjoy each daring and secret moment.

The next morning Chorus would wake her early, however deeply she slept, and they would make sure of a better view when the runners took to the track. Already there was excitement among those around her.

"Too old and too rich to defend his title!" she heard, gathering eventually that the subject of the discussion was a Sicilian who had won the sprint eight and four years earlier.

"He had quite a homecoming," announced one man, addressing anyone who might hear, "greeted by three hundred chariots, all pulled by white horses!"

Heads turned. Corinna kept hers still, avoiding eye contact.

"Three hundred horses, not chariots!"

"Chariots, I heard. I don't know how many horses."

"Whoever wins," said someone else, with deep seriousness, "will be the fastest man alive."

Such nonsense! thought Corinna. The fastest man would not be running and there was nothing to be gained by blaming anyone alive or dead. Dear Damastor. She had missed him so much. Yet for years she had barely seen him! And all the time, he was not a slave at all but the son of a citizen! If they had arrived in time to tell him who he really was, could he have registered to run?

Corinna could hardly imagine how she might tell him, if she ever found him in this place. Determined to stand, she reached for the help of Chorus, who seemed neither hot nor tired, but only concerned. Corinna's head tingled damp and cold. The stadium wavered around her. Signalling to the grass behind, Chorus took her by the wrist and started to push a way through, part-battering ram and part-mountain goat. All Corinna had to do was hold on, and follow without falling.

She was still unsteady as they reached a gap in the low wall that rimmed the stadium. Greeted from outside by a different kind of air, Corinna stepped towards it, but just for a moment, turned back to look down. There was no reason to stop and stare but something drew her eye.

What was it – a colour? An outline? A movement that caught her attention as a rabbit might catch a dog's? Deep down, many rows away, a head turned as far as it might, and for a moment she met eyes that startled. Familiar eyes that had not dared to rest on hers but at the same time disdained and discounted her. It was not until she breathed in the shade of the trees beyond the stadium that she named him. Just a slave, but the one she liked least. He would not have known her; she would not have known herself in a crowd. But had he seen Chorus, the slave woman he would not forget, who had bested and shamed him and broken his staff?

132

Theognis. Dismissing his image in her head, she let Chorus lead in search of watered wine. It was nothing. A glimpse. A heartbeat, no more. It was one thing to find a face by accident, only to lose it, and another to trace it again. He was just a slave, after all. Corinna tried to picture the citizen he attended but could recall nothing but a long neck. A distinguished man, no doubt, but nothing to them and no one to fear.

Chorus fanned her as she sat in the thin shade of an olive tree far from the densest core of the crowd. Corinna wished it might have been the sacred one in the Altis, promising her more protection than leaves could offer. Her head cooled, and sleep loosened the fear that had locked inside her. Minutes passed and Chorus saw no reason to wake her, even when she felt the change, a sense that something carried on the air was different. She only sat upright and guarded her while around them people turned to the stadium, listening when they could not see.

So Corinna did not watch Damastor take his place for the first heat of the sprint, at the starting line where stones were set firm in white sand. She did not hear the name of Lysias of Athens, son of Megacles, announced by a herald with little voice left after the competition in which he had not been placed. Lysias cleared the grin from his face as he looked around the crowd for familiar faces. He hoped that those who knew him lacked hearing acute enough to question the announcement. Lysias detected no swirl of doubt or surge of protest, and as Damastor acknowledged the crowd with the simplest grace, allowed himself to lift a short fist in the air.

Stifling a laugh, Lysias pressed the sealed hand against his chest between his ribs. Now it began, and for the first time in his life Damastor might determine his own ending. Damastor and the other athletes, with a contribution from the judges.

And the gods? Was it really in their hands? Could they work Damastor's muscles or control his mind? Wasn't the future his to shape with a few long strides? *Lion*, thought Lysias, as Damastor limbered, stretched and crouched. *Go!*

As a wave the athletes lifted and flowed down the track, one stranded within the first two strides, one limping to the side half way, and the rest forging as one but only briefly – before the cluster broke. Leaving two to straggle, sapped, and three to push on, with one alone now, and finding even at the finish a last stride that was longer and faster!

Lysias dared not leap or even stand. Damastor had won by two paces. No doubt and no dispute. The place in the final was his, and the crowd politely waited for the herald to declare his name. Lysias closed the mouth that had fallen open in astonishment in spite of the faith he had shaped as certainty. He tensed, turned his head, scanned and waited. The name was greeted only with applause. No one rose with a hand in the air. In the judges' box all sat passively, their appreciation dignified.

Still on the track, Damastor's chest lifted and sank, his breathing slowing again. His legs felt strong. He knew he might have entered the dolikhos, twelve laps long, and stood upright at the end. He walked, his mind and senses overwhelmed, assaulted, numbed, as the other athletes offered congratulations and the crowd cheered.

He looked for Lysias and a wrist waving a red cloth like a small flag announcing victory. Remembering the strip of wool blowing in the breeze outside the farmhouse in scant honour of Corinna's birth, he wondered how she would feel if she knew he mouthed her name as he thrust out his chest at the finish. And then an official gestured them off the track so that the next heat might follow swiftly. Damastor realised that for all his confidence something like shock had wrapped around him. He walked away from the stadium, the noise ebbing away with each step.

Beyond the walls that skirted the arena he felt oddly changed as he made his way through the crowd towards the stalls around the camp site. With no money for food until he found Lysias again, he recalled a fountain not so far from the Altis where he longed to lean, fill his mouth and cool his head.

So many voices, and yet he heard one through all the rest – louder than the water's gush and spray, the cries of greeting or the shouts of the wine sellers competing for trade. Was it the voice itself, barely raised? Or the tone, scathingly impatient, or the name it called?

"Theognis!"

Damastor saw the slave first and master second as Theognis heard and turned. He was carrying a basket laden with bread, figs, and something roasted that smoked thinly through the weave.

Placing himself to the side of the nearest stall, Damastor leaned just far enough to see the slave carry the basket towards two men intent on low-voiced conversation. All he could see of the citizen was his back, elegant enough but unremarkable. He clearly had business to conduct, and insisted that his companion take first pickings.

Damastor told himself he could not know. He had concluded in haste. But still he felt the certainty. The neck did not turn, and offered no glimpse of the master's face. Neither did Theognis allow his eyes to wander as he stood, no doubt hungry, with the food in his arms. And then, a movement, a turn of the head, momentary but enough. A profile, not noble enough for a sculptor, but carved in his memory. Thasos. The owner a slave like Theognis was born to serve!

Perhaps it was only for transactions such as these that Thasos was here. Would he have further meetings scheduled for the morning, more urgent than the sprint final in the stadium? Or might he choose the grunts, trips and combat of the wrestling when the pentathlon began? And if a stray javelin should pin him to the ground like a bird ready for plucking, who would mourn? Not his bride-to-be, spared the cage where she would lose the heart to sing. Corinna. Men were murdered for a great deal less.

Damastor edged away towards the Altis, and wondered what Zeus would make of it all. But he could only focus on the finish. Lysias was the thinker. Drinking from the fountain at last, Damastor let the water splash over his head and trickle onto his shoulders. The gods would be with them; it was not for him to doubt. He would make his way to the trees at the furthest point of the site and find a place to run, and run, and rest, and eat, and wake and exercise and run again. It was all he could do.

Chapter Sixteen

Lysias had never known a longer night. He hoped Damastor had slept, oblivious to his restlessness, counting on him. But to do what? He felt exposed. The tactician was no more than a dreamer after all. And all it took to thwart him was the presence of the wrong man. Or two.

The morning felt oddly unremarkable as they prepared, as far away as possible from the atmosphere that would soon begin to build. Damastor asked no questions, his focus on the body that must respond when the brain gave the signal. Lysias wished he had answers that did not involve strangulation or poison. But were Thasos and Theognis really the problem, or merely a distraction?

He heard the birdsong as never before. But then it was too early for anyone else but the most hard-working of stall holders. They were possessed, the pair of them. He could not be sure where the madness would drive them, and it was his fault, his alone!

All the time he kept up the usual encouragement, the counting, the nagging, the praise, while Damastor exercised, ran a little and practised the start. And by the time other athletes and trainers began to play the same parts in their own routines, he knew the sacrifice that must be made, not to Zeus but to necessity. It was not so enormous. Only emotion made it so. It was simply the first step without which others could not be taken. As they ate and drank he told Damastor he would not be there to see him win.

"I am needed elsewhere."

"You will bind and gag them both," asked Damastor, "and tie them to the furthest tree?"

Lysias grinned, and wiped the porridge that dripped to his chin.

"That's it!" he cried. "The solution!"

But seeing Damastor looking anxious, he continued, "Focus. Lion and prey. The rest is not your concern but mine." He added that although he had been trained as a soldier he would need only his brain.

Damastor allowed himself to feel reassured. There was a part of him that had not woken from a different world. He had dreamed not of races or olive wreaths but Corinna. Looking at Lysias, who loved her too, he wondered whether he would ever be able to tell him.

Not now, he told himself, as he pictured her rising to her feet and throwing her arms in the air. She was far away and only in his dream could he lean silently to smooth away her hair and place his lips on her forehead. Lysias had finished his breakfast and drained his wine. He stood, full of purpose.

"You must go now?"

"Yes, and steal a cloak. May the gods be with us both."

They had never embraced before. As Damastor watched Lysias make his way through the crowd towards the camp site, he realised he was alone.

Chorus had pointed in the direction of the field events, and Corinna had wondered whether she would have preferred to watch the javelin throwers. They sat in the stadium already, among the earliest to arrive. This time they would be close enough, thanks to her wide-awake determination, for a view of the finish as the sprinters lunged. It felt important to see the second fastest man alive. But would Damastor be watching? And where was Lysias? She shook her head at her own stupidity. They would be training, of course, with horses and chariot, and both of them so much further away than she had ever imagined. It seemed to Corinna that the valley was more than big enough for a few armies, and their families too.

She had not forgotten Theognis, and asked herself who might have bought him from her father. But the surprise was that she had seen him at all. It was surely impossible that among so many people gathering on all sides, they would ever meet face to face. She must dismiss all thoughts of everything and everyone but the excitement, the spectacle – and the pretence. Her voice, when she was forced to use one, must be deep. And she must address Chorus as Father. It felt like a game, but as her mother had impressed upon her, one that would be no fun at all if they found themselves discovered and forcibly ejected from the site. She might be a youth now, but she must be silent as a woman.

Around her, others were pointing to the rows near the judges' box where the famous were rumoured to take advantage of reserved seats. Someone had arrived with escorts; Corinna had no idea who he might be. All she could see was a man who considered himself worthy of fuss and fawning. Although she heard a name, it carried no meaning, and less interest than a flower she might try to identify. When Chorus asked with her hands, Corinna answered with a shrug, and for the first time felt like a real boy, trying out a swing of the legs.

But something else was happening, and the celebrity was forgotten already. Below, preparations were underway on the track. Five stakes were carried like short spears by officials walking perfectly in step. Corinna watched the first pressed down hard into the white ground beside the pebbles that marked the start. Another had to be hammered firmly at the finish, at the end of the straight before the oval track looped round. Between the two, three others were being placed at carefully measured intervals. Although she avoided the eyes of anyone but Chorus, Corinna made good use of her ears. The track was wide enough, it seemed, for twenty athletes, but the sprint was for eight finalists. The favourite to win, based on his performance in the heats, seemed to be an Athenian with the same name as her brother.

Corinna smiled to imagine her Lysias running, chest out like a stallion but his legs splaying and stumbling like an injured goat. Impatiently, she wondered when the athletes would appear and she would see this favourite for herself.

Lysias was beginning to think that even with a cohort of foot soldiers strategically placed, he might have been destined to fail. The camp site was emptying now, and the stalls running out of hot food, but he had not found Thasos, though he had tried the most expensive accommodation and the most impressive pavilions. He had asked any citizen who seemed, by his dress and manner, to consider himself sufficiently important to be the acquaintance of such a great man. But soon the competition would begin, in the races and the field events, and still he had found no one who had seen him. Standing at the main entrance to the stadium, he watched those who filed in, but in vain. Soon it would be too late, and he would have to wait and see, and hope – that Thasos would applaud a slave he wanted dead as he ran to victory!

"Lysias? I heard you were to race a chariot!"

The voice came from behind. The last time Lysias had heard it had been in a court of law, and Damastor had been on trial. Now he felt the narrowed eyes of Theognis as he turned to greet the man who intended to marry his sister.

The gods smiled down! Lysias smiled too, as gracious and charming as he knew how to be – and as respectful. How honoured he was! What a happy and fortuitous encounter, since he had been looking for Thasos in the hope of spending some time in his company!

It was hard to tell whether Thasos was flattered or taken aback. While Lysias talked, probably too much and with excessive animation, about the prospect of seeing the early stages of the pentathlon, he simply listened. Lysias watched his face. No figure on a jar could be flatter, less mobile or responsive. Then there came a point when he feared he must stop and let silence herald whatever answer might follow. Dare he take his arm? And would it be warm, or cool as marble?

"I understand the sprint has been delayed but if you are eager not to miss it, we can return later. I have a particular interest in the wrestling. I would be glad to introduce you to Pheidias, a champion at the last Olympiad and still considered by some the favourite, since I had the honour to learn from him at the gymnasion."

Thasos lifted his eyebrows. Someone had told Lysias that the Olympiad was a perfect place for spotting the celebrated, but he had not guessed that all he needed to lure and secure Thasos was a famous friend! As he talked, Lysias moved away from the stadium, reaching out one arm out like a host welcoming a valued guest, ushering with due deference. Thasos was walking within its arc, and Theognis a step behind. Afraid to pause, physically or verbally, Lysias kept on walking, grateful for the first nod and murmur. It was followed by an "Indeed?" as they moved further from the track and closer to the grass where the wrestlers were waiting for the pankration to begin.

Thasos smiled his appreciation at the sight of them. Arms swinging, waist bent or leg muscles stretched, they gathered like a city wall that would take some battering. Seeing Pheidias, and certain Pheidias could not see him, Lysias pointed him out to Thasos and raised his hand in greeting. From that distance Pheidias would not know his mother from a thorn bush.

"Isn't it all-out combat by another name?" asked Thasos, and Lysias thought he detected in his eyes a sudden brightness. "In defeat, what's lost is consciousness, is it not?"

Lysias believed that the rules had been changed to reduce the likelihood of mutilation. A concussed opponent was no longer the goal, any more than the separation of eyes from their sockets. But there was no need to disappoint Thasos now that for the first time his face had softened into something like a smile.

In the stadium the crowd became suddenly subdued. Corinna leaned to the side of a man with a thick neck and an annoying habit of moving his head more often than a quail. She looked to Chorus, who nodded and pointed. The crowd cheered. The competitors for the sprint were arriving on the track. Corinna could see there was a line of them, and that all of them, bar one, were tall, as tall as Damastor. Colour alone suggested they were naked. But fidget and squint as she might she was simply too short to be sure, her view in every direction blocked by men with large heads and broad backs. Chorus tapped the shoulder of the biggest problem in front of her. At once the head turned. Chorus pressed her hands down in air. No smile. Just an expectation. The man stared, affronted for a moment, before sliding down obediently in his seat.

Corinna smiled her thanks as, like a frieze, the scene below was revealed. Then her lips parted in a sound that was not quite a word. The name she heard from the herald was her brother's name, and the athlete who bowed at the sound of it was Damastor.

"In the name of Hera," she murmured, and sank low in her seat.

Chorus furrowed her brow. Corinna touched her chest where the heart beat. Briefly she cradled her arms around an invisible baby. Then she sucked in her lips, as if afraid of what might escape from her mouth. Chorus frowned as she stared. The runners were preparing, keeping their long limbs loose.

Among the crowd she felt a change, a final stir that like a gust of wind soon dropped to stillness. Corinna looked to Chorus and found her large hands meeting in a knot, her eyes intent. But surely she was looking not at Damastor, but another runner whose name Corinna could not recall. Perhaps she was struck by his colour, for he was not pale or brown but red as a watermelon. In height and build he and Damastor were very much alike, the way he walked with his hands on his hipbones oddly similar.

Corinna pointed to Damastor, but still Chorus fixed her gaze on the athlete with the strangely red skin. Of course, Corinna realised, she could not recognise Damastor after twenty years. Nor did she understand; how could she? But what did it mean? What did they do to impostors? Corinna let loose a sigh that quivered.

The signal sounded. The eight finalists took their places on the starting line. Damastor was ready. He met the glance of the athlete to his left, announced as Melissus of Athens, son of Archilochus. The look was hard to read – not hostile, but neither was it a smile. His skin was so raw he might have spent the night tossed in brambles, but his shoulders were strong.

Damastor looked away, eyes ahead. No distractions. But had he seen this man before? He would remember. Perhaps the man had seen him. Was it disbelief he read in the sore red face? Damastor looked left again. Melissus of Athens turned away. Damastor tensed. Lion, he heard Lysias murmur. Prey. Nothing else. Go.

Run, Damastor! Fly! Corinna's neck was as high as she could lift it, her chest leaning forward, her thighs clinging to the front of the seat while her backside parted from the rest. Stones from a sling! Such force and so instant! And then the short Cretan was shouldering through the rest like a bull between horses. But only for a breath! There was no more than the length of an elbow between any of the athletes as they passed the first stake. It was hard, as they moved, to hold on to Damastor, towering a foot's length behind the Cretan. Stride for stride, he and Melissus raced as one, as if linked by an invisible mechanism. Together they edged ahead, or did they? Still the Cretan held his ground between them, head down as they passed the fourth stake, the three of them apart from the rest. The Cretan's pace slowed. He was wading now, his head rocking. Only two could win – two like palms of the same hand, paired but for thin air wedged between them.

Corinna stretched as she leaned, her view shuttered out by rising shoulders. And Damastor's final stride hurtled him – head first, arms grasping, almost toppling – past the stake, a pace ahead! Surely? Had he won? Were the roars for him?

Damastor looked around him at the athletes. Some folded at the waist; others were still but for their chests swelling and falling, and some were walking, holding straight but slow. All were listening, heads up or down but waiting for the verdict of the judges. Melissus, son of Archilochus, crossed towards him, breathing hard but stepping lightly, and shook his hand. Again Damastor felt something in his scrutiny that was more than curiosity but not quite recognition. His grip was dry, a gritty crispness under Damastor's palm. Their heads were close, their breathing falling into the same rhythm as he murmured in Damastor's ear.

"Well done, whoever you are."

Damastor saw the official with the laurel wreath advancing. But towards which of them was he heading? Into a sudden silence the trumpet burst, faltering. Then it scaled up triumphantly, as if to reach the clouds. The herald stood beside the trumpeter, ready to make his announcement.

"The winner is Lysias of Athens, son of Megacles."

For the crowd it was over. Second and third meant nothing, and as the wreath was laid around Damastor's bowed head, the names of Melissus and the Cretan were buried beneath a sound unlike any other he had heard. It was made up of voices and feet and hands, and it was dense and jubilant, and all for him.

Corinna stood as others stood, peering in vain until Chorus lifted her under her arms like a puppy with legs hanging. As she lowered her to the ground again Corinna smiled her thanks, and sank into her seat as if she and not Damastor had run the sprint, and lost the strength to stand.

Damastor saw Melissus lifting his own hands as if to show him what to do. Arms high, he acknowledged the cheers, facing the crowd on each side, and still they cheered, again and again, an endless, throbbing sound from all around him, a sound that must surely be heard by the gods on Mount Olympus.

As it reached the green where the first two wrestlers knotted and grunted, Thasos and Theognis turned towards it. Lysias did not wait for the question. Time to be gone! Quickly he ducked behind a mound of flesh provided by a group of trainers and their pentathletes. He slipped into hiding, waiting only a moment before he ran as best he could, between bodies and trees, to the wall around the stadium. At the gap through which a few spectators were leaving, he heard his own name as if on the wind. From the top and back of the seating he could see little but figures, mainly official, and one naked but for an olive wreath. Then with an escort of honour, and pelted with flowers, the winner left the stadium and the noise subsided at last. Damastor! He had won. Of course he had won! And now Lysias knew it was up to him.

But should it be now and at once? Dared he wait, until the presentation of vats of oil and torrents of drachma, the promise of tax that need not be paid and the best seats in the theatre for as long as the champion lived? How long could it be before Thasos heard the same name carried out to the field, and marched in the cause of justice to the judges' box?

If it was to be a race then he must win it. Against the flow of several hundred people leaving their seats, Lysias made his way, pushing, apologising, thrusting, dodging and weaving, down to the arena and the entrance where only athletes and officials were allowed to gather and emerge. There were guards of a kind but they were not prepared for an unarmed ambush. Lysias broke past them and looked up to the box where the judges sat like princes on cushions. As officials ran towards him from all directions, he took up position by the fifth stake, pulled it from the ground with a ferocious tug and raised it high.

"I am Lysias of Athens, son of Megacles!"

Into the silence boos and groans were scattered. He raised his hand. Where was Damastor? He needed him by his side.

"The victor of the stadion race," he paused, looking for him through the gathered group of agitated men in white, "is not a citizen, but a slave."

What was it he heard this time? Shock? Disbelief? Anger – but against whom? And was that Thasos at the back of the stadium, looking down and raising a hand?

"A cheat and an impostor!" came the cry from above. It was thin and brittle but travelled like a javelin, one that broke a record and left the crowd stunned.

"The winner," cried Lysias, "clear and undisputed, in a fair race well run! Because, citizens, you and I were not born with sharper minds or finer sensibilities than the slaves we buy and sell like couches to lean on! Not all of us, as your eyes will tell you, were even born more handsome!"

A jeer. Another. But there he was, the slave in question! Damastor strode through to join him, and no one attempted to hold him back. Lysias took Damastor's left arm and raised it high in the silence that clung again.

"Here is the proof! His name is Damastor and he is the fastest man alive. Each of you has witnessed it and cannot deny the evidence before you! When we are born to be citizens we are not born faster. Neither are we stronger or braver, but only more fortunate."

He paused. Whatever might be happening in the judges' box no one moved to carry him away.

"Damastor and I were boys together. I grew up with the promise of respect. Did I need to earn it? I did not! Did this slave deserve all the respect Athens has always denied him? Yes, he did! And not, citizens, because of his speed alone, but because of his courage and endurance." Lysias paused, measuring his hold on an audience now hushed. "Respect, because his power lies not only in his legs but in the strength of his spirit. And because he is as honourable as any citizen in this stadium."

A cheer? A single cheer, young and high. A father and son seemed to be on their feet. But behind them Thasos was not finished.

"Flog him!"

It was one voice but at once they heard it echoed. Glancing up, Lysias saw movement in the judges' box. Some kind of sign? The officials moved too, encircling Lysias and Damastor, taking them by the arms.

"Honour him, citizens!" cried Lysias. "Remember him, and the lie that today you saw stripped bare! Honour Damastor – and let the truth set us free!"

The words were the last he could share with the crowd. But he had not finished. He must address those who led and surrounded them.

"Damastor followed my orders as always, as duty obliged him to do, and with absolute loyalty!" he declared, though the men did not meet his eyes and showed no signs of hearing. "He is blameless and any punishment must be mine!"

Damastor turned. Beside him Lysias had never felt so small. Corinna was trembling. A sob escaped as the prisoners were led away. Guarded like a tax collector who had cheated all of Attica, but with no shield to protect him from spittle, Damastor was escorted with Lysias, as quickly as the crowd allowed, towards the Bouleuterion.

Corinna must make Chorus understand. She could not do this alone, whatever it might be. But Chorus was standing already, and expecting her to follow. While a trumpeter sounded a warning that another race was about to begin, they made their way through an unsettled crowd that talked and turned, heads shaking in disbelief. Were they of one mind, and did that mind belong to Thasos? Corinna could not be sure.

She felt only the disturbance, its edges sharp and its note off-key. Might it break into debate, or only unite in outraged hostility against the two men she loved most?

She must run to keep up with Chorus, but where was she going? And was that Damastor ahead, where the crowd gathered like dogs around a fallen bird? The door of the Bouleuterion was closing. Chorus barged in, dragging Corinna by the wrist behind her.

Chapter Seventeen

Lysias looked to Damastor as the door closed. It was a wordless appeal, and Damastor answered it by taking his hand. He clasped it firmly. Someone held out an arm in front of Chorus, but Corinna was afraid she would knock it away.

"Why are you here?" asked the man, as Chorus narrowed her eyes.

Unable to meet the stare that fixed him, he looked nervously to a higher authority for support.

"Because Lysias means only the best for Damastor!" cried Corinna, urging more power into her voice, "but he does not know the whole truth – could not begin – and the judges must hear it all."

The group of officials who had clustered around her brother and Damastor opened up as she spoke. She stepped closer to them. The heads that turned now looked down on her.

"My name is Corinna."

She waited. She needed to see his face, his mouth opening, and his shoulders falling, his eyes full as they met hers. His mouth shaped her name. It was silent but clear.

"Sister," murmured Lysias.

He saw that his astonishment was shared by the representatives of the Hellenodikai and the head judge who had left the box in the stadium to examine the case. One of them gestured to a table around which they all took a place.

Then the judge held out a hand to Corinna, an invitation to continue. But outside the door someone was knocking, not once, but twice, three times, again, and louder. Lysias heard a voice he had been expecting. Thasos. With furious urgency he announced his name as if all doors should open at the sound of it.

"Sirs," said Lysias, "the citizen you hear is betrothed to my sister Corinna, but not yet entitled to intervene in her business. He has no knowledge of any bearing on this matter."

The officials conferred as Corinna looked to the door and winced at another knock, even louder than before. Damastor's smile willed her on. They must listen, not to Thasos, but to her.

"Continue," said the judge, and nodded to Corinna.

She linked her hands and gripped them tightly.

"I am the daughter of Megacles of Athens and his wife, the wise and gentle Alcestis. My brother Lysias wants the world to be more just and equal, and I applaud him, as I applaud Damastor, the fastest man alive."

Someone clapped. It wasn't Lysias, though he joined in. The applause came from the athlete Damastor had defeated so narrowly. Melissus stood at the back, a chiton covering him now but his face crusted red. Corinna faltered. But she had not finished.

"The truth that neither of them knows, since it has only recently been uncovered, is that Damastor is not by birth a slave at all. He is the son of a citizen, abandoned by a citizen's wife and exposed on a hillside. My father found him, and took pity on him."

Corinna could no longer look at Damastor. She felt as though there was a line she must try to hold, and it would slip through her fingers if she allowed herself to feel what he might feel.

"This is Chorus, his mother's trusted slave," she continued, "who followed her orders and carried him in a pot of clay."

She pulled Chorus forward by the hand. Looking steadily at Corinna and then around her, Chorus bowed – not to the officials, or to Damastor, but to Melissus. He stepped towards her and placed a hand on her broad shoulder.

"His mother Eurycleia was misled by a soothsayer," Melissus began, his voice failing. He cleared his throat and repeated the words, louder now. "She was sorely troubled, and suffered much while she lived. She was my mother too."

Melissus reached out to Damastor and took his hand in his.

"This is my brother, and I am proud to stand beside him. Or," he smiled, "just a little behind."

When the door opened to allow Damastor, Lysias, Corinna and Melissus to leave the Bouleuterion, Theognis was leaning against the wall outside, more like a street seller than a sentry. He straightened and looked back into the crowd.

"Where's your master?" asked Lysias. "I need to explain that he must look for another wife."

Damastor smiled at Corinna. Theognis gazed in the direction of the pavilions and shrugged.

With a kiss on the forehead for his sister, Lysias set off to find Thasos and share the news that would soon be on a thousand lips. Damastor felt Corinna slip a hand into his. Theognis snorted.

"Thasos will give thanks," he muttered. "He wouldn't marry *her* for the biggest dowry in Greece." He looked Corinna up and down. "Or is it *him*?"

As his eyes lifted again in a leer that met hers, Damastor grabbed him by the waist and threw him over his shoulder. With a thud he landed on worn grass and tipped over into horse dung that was still fresh enough to squash and smear. Melissus directed him to the nearest fountain and Damastor took Corinna's hand.

"Will it be all right?" she asked.

"It will," he said, and believed it.

There was evidence to be considered and documentation to be provided. The Hellekonidai sent to Athens for Megacles. Meanwhile a doctor examined the winner and runner-up of the stadion race and declared many similarities to support kinship. The head judge, who had presided over three Olympiads, initiated a search of the archives which uncovered a victor in the female Games for Hera by the name of Eurycleia, who won the sprint as an unmarried girl. Pheidias, as yet unbeaten in the Pankration, vouched for Lysias – once he had moved close enough to throw him over his shoulder as he had more than once seen fit to do.

The result was amended but upheld. The winner of the stadion race was Damastor of Athens, younger son of Archilochus, who had defeated his brother Melissus by a stride.

Before the crowd dispersed from the stadium at the end of the day's events, Damastor and Melissus were presented once again. This time Lysias did not join them. Banned like his sister, he listened with her in the pavilion where she had been asked to retire in comfort until Megacles arrived. Lysias knew the head judge would be offering the briefest of explanations: a misunderstanding, and now a correction. But neither of them heard what was said. Only when the announcement was made did they hear from the stadium a surge of sound, louder than before, as once again the crowd acclaimed Damastor. With a smile for her brother, Corinna pictured the fastest man alive, dressed for the first time like a citizen, and waving at the sound of his own name.

Late that evening, Lysias and Damastor drank with Melissus, their eyes on the temple of Zeus, and talked a little.

"I remember you from my father's funeral," Melissus said.

"I haven't grown much," grinned Lysias, but he guessed that the memory haunted them both.

"Do you remember my uncle?" asked Melissus.

"The one who gave the oration?"

Melissus nodded and explained that it was he who had never given up searching for him, found him alone and restored him to the phatria.

"He is not well enough to travel," he added, "but he will be glad to meet my brother." He smiled at Damastor. "We have cousins too."

Damastor had no objection to cousins if they had no objection to him. He would have swapped a cohort of them for an image in his head of a mother. But what would it be? A crazed woman abandoning her baby? Or a girl, no older than Corinna, running to victory?

There were many stories to be heard, but Damastor could only guess at those his new brother seemed unwilling to tell. Lysias too was aware of them in the silences. With no wish to ask questions, about the mother, that the sons would rather not answer, he found himself strangely short of words. Kicking a small stone with the stub of his sandal, he looked around him at the other drinkers, the stall sellers clearing their wares to begin again at dawn, and the jugglers giving up all hope of impressing an audience by twilight. And Elis seemed full of dust and smoke, sweat and stupidity, and statues with bird excrement streaking their shoulders.

"Your spirits are low, Lysias?" Melissus asked him.

"He wanted a different victory," said Damastor.

He laid a hand on his back the way he used to, when as small boys they recognised no difference between them that made any sense, and crouched together to look at something that grew or crawled.

"It'll be forgotten – your part, I mean," said Melissus, "quickly enough."

Knowing that was exactly what Lysias feared, Damastor smiled his sympathy.

"My attempt to subvert justice and overturn society?" asked Lysias. "My disgrace?" He managed a wry grin. "Of course. I lost. Only winners are remembered, and that's as it should be."

They wandered together in the twilight, bought leftover food, and looked at the statues of the victors. Melissus asked Damastor where he'd like his to be. Damastor only smiled, and looked across to the pavilions, wondering whether Corinna might be thinking of him as he thought of her.

"I didn't want you to be a slave," Lysias told him, the words difficult to grasp.

He was tired. It was over but it was not, after all, as he had planned it would be, and whether the outcome was better or worse he was too exhausted to decide.

"Lysias, I know," Damastor told him.

"I only wanted you to be who you are, and valued because of that self which is deep within you. Because of the way you live, as well as run. Because you are Greek, yes, but most of all because you are human – and thus entitled to the same respect, whether citizen or slave. Because slavery degrades us all."

He remembered the saliva hurled as spit and the flogging that seemed to some of this crowd a fitting response to his big idea.

Damastor laid a hand on his shoulder.

"You are the same now as you were yesterday," Lysias told him. "You won a race but you are not a god. You will no longer obey orders but give your own, and you will do so with the same grace you have always shown, the same dignity…"

"I hope I shall," said Damastor.

"It's a different truth I hoped to share, that's all."

"If you believe it, you must keep sharing it," said Melissus.

"Until they listen? Will they ever be ready to hear?"

"Not yet, perhaps," said Melissus. "One day."

Damastor did not know. He was thinking of Corinna, her short hair, her wide eyes, and the speech she made for him. Would she ever be ready to hear the truth he had hidden from her?

"Lysias," he said, "I love your sister."

He was surprised by the laugh that followed the pause.

"Of course you do!" cried Lysias. He looked at the centre of the temple where Zeus sat enthroned and pictured him laughing too. "Hail Zeus indeed."

In the pavilion Corinna lay in comfort yet could not sleep.

"I love him, Chorus," she whispered.

She had not allowed the slave to sleep outside, where grass had been worn to dirt. In the pavilion Corinna could not see her, but heard her breathing close by, and not for the first time, felt comforted by her presence. Of course Chorus could neither hear her nor reply. But it seemed important to tell her all the same.

She heard her stir, and perhaps roll over, a sleepy grunt her only communication. Corinna smiled, realising she might laugh aloud like her brother without waking Chorus or alarming her in the least.

"I shall be a bride after all," she said, and pictured Damastor through a veil, sitting beside her in a chariot by torchlight. She imagined his mouth on her hand, her cheek, his lips closing soft and warm on hers. "Eros and Psyche, just as Eurycleia said."

Had the dark-eyed priestess seen the future after all? Or was it a wish, a penance, a stab of light in darkness? Corinna forgave Eurycleia, and asked Aphrodite to grant her peace.

Chorus was not used to a mattress so firm and at the same time so soft. It was hard to settle, and harder than usual to make sense of much that had taken place. Chorus found the past easier to understand than a present that would not stand still. She trusted in time to reveal what it might, and memory to fill the space. Feelings made safe at last.

Eurycleia: the girl she had served. Quick feet, quick hands, quick to cry. Victory at the Games for Hera, but little praise and little joy. The girl bride who could not run away. Chorus remembered the way she had talked to her, her lips so full and silent, as she showed her all her favourite jewels and combs, ribbons and mirrors – needing her there. Secret dancing by torchlight. So many secrets in a dumb slave's care.

Her eyes closed, Chorus could still see Eurycleia. How she looked, so long ago – at the slave, the tall one, who saw her when her husband was blind as stone. A young man, fast enough to catch her, and kind too – even with the man-woman deaf-mute teased by the rest.

Secret meetings. Eyes bright with fear. And look-out duty for the guard who could never tell.

A baby boy with red skin that bled to the touch – the bad fruit of secret love. Tears and guilt and the madness beginning.

And then the belly fat again. The slave lover sold by the stone husband, still blind to all but profit. The mistress weeping, with a knife to her own throat.

A soothsayer smuggled in by night, and another baby hauled out like a lamb from a ewe, cleaned but not shown, not fed, not dandled. The clay pot on the hillside.

It was over now. She was free.